Books in the Dragonflight Series

LETTERS FROM ATLANTIS
by Robert Silverberg

THE DREAMING PLACE
by Charles de Lint

THE DREAMING PLACE

CHARLES DE LINT

Illustrated by
BRIAN FROUD

A Byron Preiss Book

Atheneum 1990 New York

Collier Macmillan Canada
Toronto

Maxwell Macmillan International Publishing Group
New York   Oxford   Singapore   Sydney

THE DREAMING PLACE
Dragonflight Books

THE DREAMING PLACE Copyright © 1990 by Byron Preiss Visual
Publications, Inc.
Text copyright © 1990 by Charles de Lint
Illustrations copyright © 1990 Byron Preiss Visual
Publications, Inc.

Cover painting by Brian Froud
Book design by Robert Gould and Paula Keller
Book edited by David M. Harris

Grateful acknowledgments are made to Jane Leverick for the use of a
quote from "Dream Time," which first appeared in The Minstrel, Vol. 2,
No. 5; Lammas, 1989. Copyright © 1989 by Jane Leverick; reprinted
by permission of the author.

Special thanks to Jonathan Lanman, Richard Curtis, David Keller,
and Alice Alfonsi

Library of Congress Cataloging-in-Publication Data

De Lint, Charles, 1951–
    The dreaming place/by Charles de Lint; illustrated by Brian Froud.—1st ed.
        p.   cm.
    Summary: When a manitou, a winter earth spirit that is withering and in need of
blood, fastens upon Nina, her sixteen-year-old cousin Ash enters the Otherworld to
stop the spirit.
    ISBN 0-689-31571-6
    [1. Supernatural—Fiction.   2. Cousins—Fiction.]   I. Froud, Brian, ill.   II. title.
PZ7.D33954Dr   1990
[Fic]—dc20   90-488
                                                                                                CIP
                                                                                                AC

Atheneum
Macmillan Publishing Company
866 Third Avenue, New York, NY 10022

Collier Macmillan Canada, Inc.
1200 Eglinton Avenue East
Suite 200
Don Mills, Ontario M3C 3N1
First Edition
Printed in the United States of America

10 9 8 7 6 5 4 3 2 1

For
Kirsty & Katie

Walking with Spirits
through murals of mist
I visit my totem
in the Dreaming Place.

—Jane Leverick,
from "Dream Time"

NINA

"I didn't see you at school today, Nina," Judy said. "Were you sick?"

"No. I just couldn't go in."

"Well, I wish you'd tell me when you're going to skip. I was looking for you all over. The Tank and her crew ended up sitting at my table for lunch and I could've just died."

"Why didn't you just get up and leave?"

"Why should I? I was there first. Besides, I thought you or Laurie'd show up to rescue me, only she wasn't at school today either. How come you were playing hooky, anyway?"

"I had another one of those dreams again last night, and I just couldn't face going in."

Judy giggled. "What were you this time? An elephant?"

"It's not funny."

"I know. I'm sorry. What were you *this* time?"

"A rabbit. One of those little miniature bunnies you see hanging out on the common by Butler U."

If she looked between her sneakers, which were propped up on the windowsill, Nina Caraballo could see the ornate bell tower of Meggernie Hall from her bedroom window. It stood on University Hill, overlooking the campus and the park where last night she'd dreamed—

* * *

Her body felt all wrong. Disproportionate. Her point of view was far too low—like she was lying on the grass—except she knew she was sitting up. Her peripheral vision was so broad she could almost see behind herself. Her nose kept twitching and she could smell everything out there in the night. Newly cut grass. The sweet pungency of the lilac bushes nearby. A fascinating odor that rose from a discarded candy wrapper.

She started over to investigate it and fell all over herself in a tumble of limbs. Rear legs too long and awkward, front legs too short. A sound came from her throat that sounded far too much like the squeal of a pig for her liking. Lying there, sprawled in the grass, she could have cried.

Because she knew.

This was another one of those horrible dreams.

Clumsily, she righted herself and looked around. And found herself beginning to clean herself, licking at the soft fur of one shoulder with a pink tongue.

She immediately stopped, disgusted at the action.

"I want to wake up!" she cried.

The words came from her throat in another squeal.

Followed by silence.

But not a complete silence. Her long ears perked up as she heard rustling footsteps in the grass. She turned her head to see a massive shadowy shape approaching her cautiously from across the common.

She froze, petrified with fear.

It was a huge mastiff. A monster of a dog that she'd have avoided even if she were in her own body.

The mastiff paused when it realized she had noticed it. Through some quirk of her borrowed body's eyesight, when it stopped moving, it became almost invisible to her. She stared harder, trying to make it out, heart thumping double-time in her tiny chest. The sweep of the lawn and the mastiff's bulk all blurred into one indecipherable shadow.

Until the dog charged her.

Its growl froze her for long heartbeats more, then she bolted.

Or tried to.

Unaccustomed to the odd shape of her limbs and their correlation to each other, she went sprawling again. Before she could recover, the mastiff was rearing over her. Its jaws closed on her, capturing her tiny body, grinding bones against each other as it bit down on her flesh—

*   *   *

2

"And then I woke up," she said.

"Oh, that's gross," Judy said. "Did you really feel yourself *die*? I've heard that if you die in a dream, you die for real."

Nina shifted the phone receiver from one ear to the other.

"But that's not the worst of it," she said. "This time I've got proof that it's Ashley who's hexing me."

Judy laughed nervously. "Come *on*. You can't really believe that."

"I saw her," Nina said.

She woke in her own bed, drenched in sweat and tangled up in her bedclothes. Her relief was immediate. The dreams might keep coming— once a week or so—but they were still only dreams.

Not real.

She hadn't almost died out there in the common while trapped in the shape of an animal.

Not really.

But still. They seemed so real.

She shivered with a sudden chill and thought she could see her breath for a moment. It was so cold you'd almost think it was still winter. She exhaled experimentally, but couldn't really see her breath. The room seemed far warmer already, and she realized that her trembling chill was just a residue of her dream.

Her stupid dream.

Which wasn't real. Everybody had dreams.

She glanced across the bedroom then to see that her cousin's bed was empty. Still shaking, she got up and shuffled across the floor, arms hugged around her thin chest, to look down the hallway that lay outside their room. At the far end of the short hall, the bathroom door stood open. The light was off. There was no one inside.

It was past midnight, so why wasn't Ashley in her bed?

She tiptoed past her parents' bedroom and crept down the stairs, avoiding the third and seventh steps, both of which she knew would creak alarmingly. Halfway down, she could make out a dim glow that was coming from the living room. Because her mother's beaded curtain hung across the doorway, it wasn't until she was directly outside the room that she could properly see in.

There was Ashley, sitting cross-legged on the floor in front of the fake mantelpiece. Her dyed black hair stood up three inches from the top of her head and hung in shagged layers down her back, and she was wearing one of her typical headbanger T-shirts—not her usual tight, torn ones, but an oversized Metallica shirt that she used as a nightgown. By the light of a candle that she had placed on the end of the coffee table, she was reading a book. Nina couldn't see the title, but she didn't doubt it was one of those creepy black-magic books of which her cousin was so enamored.

Sensing her presence, Ashley looked up, her gaze locking on Nina's through the beaded curtain. A smile that was more a sneer touched her lips, and then she returned to her book, ignoring Nina's presence.

Nina fled back to their bedroom.

"But that doesn't mean anything," Judy said. "Just because she's weird doesn't mean she's a witch."

"What else would she be doing down there in the dark?" Nina wanted to know.

"You said she had a candle."

"That makes it even worse. Witches always use candles and stuff like that for their spells. I tell you, she's hexing me. I looked through some of her books when I stayed home today, and they're all about casting spells and awful things like that."

"She's just trying to spook you," Judy said.

"Well, she's doing a really good job."

"You should talk to her about it."

Nina laughed unhappily. "I can't talk to her about *anything*. And besides, if she's not hexing me, she'd tell everybody and I wouldn't be able to show my face outside the house ever again. I'd *die* if it got out."

"I won't tell anyone."

"I know. But she would. Just for spite."

Judy sighed on the other end of the line.

"Want to watch something on TV?" she asked.

Nina knew exactly what her friend was about. Time to change the subject. Not that she minded. She'd been thinking of nothing else all day long and she was sick to death of it. It made her feel like she was going crazy.

"Sure," she said.

She got up from the chair by the window and slouched on

her bed. Leaning over, she switched on the battered twelve-inch black-and-white that was on her night table.

"What's on?"

" 'Beauty and the Beast' started around ten minutes or so ago on three."

Nina turned to the channel just in time to catch a commercial from one of the local car dealerships up on Highway 14. A fat man in an ill-fitting superhero costume was extolling the virtues of "!!Hundreds of used cars at rock-bottom prices!!"

"I hate this commercial," she said. "Friendly Ed's such a geek."

Judy laughed. "His kid's in Susie's English class, and she says he looks just like him."

"Poor kid."

Because they lived across town from each other, tuning their TVs to the same channel and making comments to each other on the phone was the closest they could come to hanging out together on a school night.

More ads—one for Diet Coke and one for tampons—finally gave way to the show, which had already begun.

"I've seen this one before," Nina said.

"Yeah, it's one of the mushy ones."

"Did you ever wonder why Catherine doesn't just go live down there with Vincent? I mean, it's such a neat place. I'd live down there in a flash."

"I always wonder where they get their electricity."

They both paused as the beast character recited a few lines of poetry.

"God, I love his voice," Judy said.

"Mmm."

"Are you going to the dance on Friday?"

"I don't think so. I don't really feel up to that kind of thing this weekend."

Judy laughed. "Which means you didn't get a date either. We could go together."

And stand around like a couple of geeks, like they had at the last school dance, Nina thought.

"My dad says we make guys nervous because we're too

brainy," she said. "Girls aren't supposed to be good at math and stuff like that."

"What did you say to him?"

"Nothing. My mum called him a pig."

"Good for her."

"He doesn't really believe that," Nina added, defending her father. "He was just telling me what guys think."

"So who needs 'em?"

Nina thought of the guy who sat in the back of the calculus class. Tim Lockley. To die for. But he never even gave her a second glance.

"I suppose," she said. "Except—"

She broke off as she heard footsteps on the stairs. It was neither her mother's light tread nor her father's heavier one.

"I've gotta go," she said. "Ashley just got in."

She hated having Ashley listen in on her phone conversations. After a quick promise to be at school tomorrow, she hung up and gave the impression of giving the television her undivided attention.

Ashley paused in the doorway of their room, decked out in all her gear. Tight faded jeans, torn at the knees. A Def Leppard T-shirt with the arms torn off. A leather jacket. Hair like a black lion's mane haloing her head.

"I can't believe you watch that garbage," she said.

Nina looked up. "What's wrong with it?"

"How long do you think that show'd last if the woman was the beast?" Ashley replied.

She took off her jacket and tossed it onto her bed and unselfconsciously began to take off the rest of her clothes—with the curtains on the window wide open so that anyone standing out on the common behind their house could get an eyeful.

Which was probably just what she wanted, Nina thought.

"Well?" Ashley asked.

Nina's only response was to turn the sound up louder on the TV.

ASH

No matter what she was doing, there was always a core of anger in Ashley Enys. She'd overheard her aunt and uncle discussing it once. Their theory was that it stemmed from her mother's death and her father's refusal to take responsibility for her.

"What would be unnatural," her uncle had said, "was if she wasn't angry. She's been uprooted from everything she knew. She feels that nobody wants her—that her mother deserted her, her father has no time for her, that we've just taken her in out of obligation. Who wouldn't feel resentful in that kind of a situation? We just have to be patient with her, that's all. She'll grow out of it."

It was a pretty theory, but Ash didn't buy it for a moment. What did her aunt and uncle know, anyway? They were just a pair of burned-out hippies who refused to accept that the sixties were gone.

Sure, it hurt that her father thought she was just so much useless baggage and didn't want her hanging around cramping his style. And even though it had been three years now since her mum had died, she still missed her terribly. She couldn't deny that she'd give anything to turn time back to that moment before her mother's death, to return to when they were living together in their little flat in St. Ives and she was going to her own school, hanging out with her own friends.

It was getting so that she was losing her accent—and with it, she felt, her identity. Culturally, North America was so far behind the way things were back home that if she went back now she'd probably feel as out of place there as she did here. But she'd return in a flash if she had the chance. She'd go back and try to put her life back on track again.

Except without Mum. . . .

It hurt, remembering. Missing what had been. Trying to imagine how things might have gone if her life hadn't been so irrevocably changed—twisted inside out on the blade of a madman's knife.

We're so sorry, everyone said, but what did they know about sorrow? What did they know about the helplessness she felt knowing that if her mother had just taken another road home from the pub that evening everything would still be fine?

But that was pain. And though it could make her angry—*did* make her angry, whenever she thought about the unfairness of it all—the constant hostility she felt seemed more deeply rooted than that. These days everything made her bristle.

And Nina made such an easy target.

They had so little in common. Her cousin was at the top of her class, which naturally made Ash's own dismal marks look even worse. Nina and her friends were all clean-cut and brainy— not exactly nerds or preppies, but not exactly cool either. Their idea of great music was Debbie Gibson; they wouldn't recognize a decent guitar riff if it grabbed them by the throat and shook them—the way all good music should. And to actually watch pap like this sucky rip-off of Cocteau's great film. . . .

She sighed as she finished undressing and put on a baggy Motley Crüe T-shirt, trying to tune out the TV's tinny sound without much luck. She put away her clothes by simply heaping them on her chair by the window, then took the book she'd bought earlier that evening out of her army-issue shoulder bag and sat up on her bed, pillows propped up against the headboard behind her.

Of course it wasn't either Nina or "Beauty and the Beast" that had her upset tonight. It was that creepy guy who'd followed her home from the occult shop downtown on her way home.

She could usually handle the guys that tried to come on to her. There were the rednecks that you just gave the finger to when they made their sleazy comments. The preppies and new wavers you ignored. Punkers and headbangers—well, you checked them out to see how interesting they were before you made up your mind to brush them off or not.

But this guy . . .

He gave her the creeps.

She couldn't place him. He was tall, with short black hair and lean features. At least three or four years older than her—he could even be twenty. He wore skinhead boots and jeans, a plain white T-shirt and a long black leather raincoat.

And he had scary eyes.

Dangerous eyes.

She'd first seen him watching her in the shop when she was buying a used copy of *The New Dimensions Red Book*, a collection of essays on the occult by Fortune, Butler, Regardie and the like. Then later, on the way home—walking, because she'd blown the last of her money on the book—she'd sensed someone following her. She'd turned around, and there he was, skulking on a street corner, standing under its light and making no attempt to hide. Just lounging there like he owned the street, watching her.

She'd taken a circuitous route through Lower Crowsea to her aunt and uncle's house where it backed on Butler U.'s common, but he'd stayed right on her heels. No closer, no farther away than he'd been when she'd first spotted him. Finally she'd just had to go into the house—letting him know where she lived—or she'd be past her curfew, which was not a good idea, considering how strict her aunt was getting with that kind of thing these days. She'd been canned last weekend—the whole weekend!—for trailing in too late on Thursday night.

Closing the door, she'd looked out the window to see him walk slowly past. He'd paused right at the end of their walk, smiled at her through the window, lips thin and feral, eyes glinting, and then gone on.

But he'd left something behind.

A promise.

She was going to see him again.

And that was what had Ash creeped out now.

She wished there was someone she could talk to about it, but she didn't have anyone. Her aunt and uncle's solution would probably be to not let her go out in the evenings anymore. The kids she hung out with would just laugh, and besides, there would go the tough rep that she worked so hard to maintain. And as for Nina . . .

She looked up to find her cousin watching her, an odd look in her eyes. For one moment she wanted to just open up to Nina, but then that unaccountable animosity reared up inside her.

"Why don't you just take a picture?" she found herself saying.

Nina quickly returned her attention to her television set. Another sigh escaped Ash, and then she opened her book and began to read the first essay, Fortune's "The Myth of the Round Table."

But as she read, the memory of the stranger's dangerous eyes sat uneasily there in the back of her mind, refusing to be forgotten.

NINA

Parents were always embarrassing, but sometimes Nina felt that hers were particularly so. They were tried-and-true holdovers from the sixties.

Her mum still wore her hair in a long braid that fell down to the small of her back and tended toward long, loose flower-print dresses and skirts. She'd first come to North America from her native England to work as a nanny, but ended up staying because the Summer of Love was in full swing, and, being a hippie at heart—though she hadn't known it before she'd come—she ended up fitting right in.

Nina's dad was half Italian and half Native American, which, her mum had confided to her once, was what had initially attracted her to him. Back then anybody who had even a flicker of Indian blood was a big deal. He was a big, broad-shouldered man with a dark complexion, small gold hoops in each ear and hair so black it seemed to swallow light. He kept it long and tied back in a ponytail. Judy once told her that he looked like a biker and she'd been scared to death of him the first time she came over to Nina's house. Now she thought he was neat.

"I wish my parents were like yours," she'd said a few weeks later in Nina's bedroom.

Her own parents were second-generation Chinese-Americans and still had funny ideas about what a kid could and couldn't do.

Extracurricular activities at school—like volleyball practice, the drama club and stuff like that—were fine so long as she kept up her good marks, but seeing boys was right out. Never mind that she was sixteen now. The only way she got out of the house on a Friday or Saturday night to go to a dance or just hang out at the mall was through various elaborate stories of visiting Nina or Susie—stories that Nina's parents, with their more open attitude, were quite happy to corroborate.

Which did make her parents sort of neat, Nina thought, but it was still embarrassing telling people that her mum made her living producing little beaded earrings and things like that, which she sold at craft fairs while her dad worked in construction, not because he didn't have the credentials for a better job, but because he'd rather "be building something than pushing mean-ingless pieces of paper around on a desk."

Nina kind of liked helping her mum out at her booth at the various craft shows, but she wished that they could just leave that whole-earth folksiness at the shows, instead of letting it take over the house as well. Everywhere you turned there were psyche-delic posters, beanbag furniture, herbs and spices hanging out to dry, record albums stored in plastic milk crates and that kind of thing. Along a wall of the living room was a brick-and-board bookcase filled with poetry of Ginsberg and Blake, a battered copy of *The Whole Earth Catalogue* and vegetarian cookbooks, hippie philosophy books like *Monday Night Class*, by a guy who only called himself "Stephen," and others by Timothy Leary, Kahlil Gibran, and Abbie Hoffman.

It was as though time had stood still for them.

On some level, Nina supposed she admired her parents for sticking to their beliefs, for living by their philosophies instead of only paying lip service to them. Politically, they leaned more toward liberalism and were involved in animal-rights issues, homes for the homeless and God knew how many environmental concern groups—all things that Nina thought were important, too. But sometimes she wished they could just have ordinary furniture, a color TV in the living room—she'd bought her own little black-and-white at a garage sale with baby-sitting money—and sit around in the backyard with soft drinks and hot dogs for a change.

But things could be worse, she supposed. Her parents could have named her Rainbow or Cloud. Or she could have Judy's parents, who were already picking out the guy they expected her to marry when she finished school. So long as Nina was reasonable about what she did, her parents gave her more freedom than a lot of other kids ever had. Like staying home from school yesterday. There were no questions asked—her parents were only worried.

"Are you sure you're ready to go back to school today?" her mum asked her when she came down for breakfast that morning.

They had the kitchen to themselves. Her dad had already left for work—he had to be on-site at seven—and Ashley had gotten up early for a change and was gone as well. Her mum would be leaving for her studio up by the market around the same time that Nina left for school.

"I'm feeling a lot better," Nina said.

At least she hadn't had that dream again last night.

"So long as you're sure."

"I'm sure."

Though if her mum really wanted her to feel better and stay better, she'd move the family from this place to a house where Nina wouldn't have to share her room with a witch. But they'd been through that before—not the witch part, just how she and Ashley didn't get along—and there was about as much chance of their moving as there was of her dad going to work in a suit and tie. They couldn't afford to move, her mother would explain, and besides, couldn't she find a little compassion for her cousin?

Compassion? Sure. Nina thought it was terrible that Ashley had lost her own mum and that her dad didn't want her. But Ashley had been living with them for three years now, and Nina's patience for her cousin had long since run its course.

Still, she knew better than to bring that up again. Instead, she asked her mother how she was coming along in her preparation for the big spring craft show, which gave them something else to talk about over breakfast.

They left together right after they'd eaten, only Nina had to go back into the house to get a jacket as soon as she stepped out onto the porch.

"Maybe I'd better take your temperature," her mother said when Nina returned wearing a jean jacket.

"Come on, Mum."

"It's not exactly cold this morning."

Nina blinked with surprise. She had goose bumps on her own arms.

"It's not?" she said.

"Maybe you should stay home another day," her mother said. "I think you've got a chill."

Hot and cold flashes, Nina thought. The sure sign of a flu. Except she hadn't been sick yesterday and she sure didn't feel sick today. Just a little chilled, and she was fine now with her jacket on.

"I'm okay," she protested. "Honest."

"Well . . ."

"I'm going to miss my bus."

Her mother sighed and allowed her better judgment to be overruled. They walked together to the corner of Grasso and Lee, where Nina caught the City Transport downtown to Redding High in midtown. Her mother kissed her good-bye and then walked on up Lee to her studio, leaving Nina only after extracting a promise that she'd return home if she started feeling sick again.

Nina slouched on a bench, doing her best to ignore the guy who was leaning up against the bus-stop sign. Danny Connick. Thin as a rake, with huge, popping eyes and always carrying a suck sack, he was the neighborhood computer nerd and, for some unknown reason, considered himself God's gift to women. He was always coming on to Nina, so naturally they had to share the same bus to school.

He kept trying to catch her eye this morning, so she looked away, hugging her jacket more tightly closed because she was starting to feel cold again.

"Hey, Nina," he called over.

She closed her eyes and pretended she didn't hear him.

"Nina!"

A chill like the icy breath of a winter wind hit her, making her gasp with surprise. She opened her eyes with a start. For one moment, she was looking at the world through a gauze of falling snow, then suddenly she was—

Elsewhere.

Out of her body. In something else's body. The feeling was too familiar for her not to recognize it. She looked down at herself to see the front legs of an alley cat, mottled and gray. Her vision was all off again: perspective wrong, peripheral vision enhanced, colors muted. A world of scents assailed her nostrils: car exhaust, garbage and litter from the alleyway. Sounds were multiplied and came too sharply—breaking in her ear like brittle crystal. She was perched on the lid of a garbage can, looking out of the alley at the bus stop—

Where she was still sitting on the bench, waiting for the bus.

A sick feeling settled in the pit of her stomach as she looked at herself from outside her body.

Please, she thought. Don't let this be real.

She wasn't even asleep this time, so how could she be dreaming?

Unless she'd fallen asleep there on the bench....

Maybe if she took the cat's body over to where her own was sitting and jumped on its lap, the contact would break the spell that had caught her. For spell was what it had to be.

Ashley's hexing.

She started forward, but, as had invariably happened to her in her dreams, the unfamiliar body moved all wrong. She lost her balance and only just caught herself from falling off the lid of the garbage can. Her frustration came out in the form of a plaintive meow.

She really didn't need this. The next time she saw Ashley, she was going to—

A buzzing started up in the back of her head—a built-in natural warning system that the cat whose body she inhabited recognized, even if she didn't. She turned slowly, careful how she moved the cat's limbs, to see the vague shape of a figure standing there at the back of the alleyway. It was too much in shadow for her to make out—too ill-defined, even seeing it through the cat's enhanced vision.

The smell of snow filled the air. And a winter chill. Frost

rimmed the brick walls and ground of the alleyway—emanating from the figure, where it lay thickest.

The figure spoke, but Nina couldn't make out what it said. She heard only the sound of its voice—low and gravelly, like the sound of ice shifting and cracking on a river's frozen surface.

What do you want? Nina tried to ask, for she knew that the figure wanted something from her, but all that issued forth from the cat's throat was a strangled sound.

The figure took a step forward.

Nina felt the cold deepen. She thought she could see snow in the air. She heard a clicking sound—like the beads of her mother's curtain moving against each other, only softer.

Then the cat's spirit reared up in panic and took over its body again. It turned and sprang away with heart-wrenching speed that would have made Nina's stomach lurch—if she'd had her own stomach. If she wasn't just some disembodied spirit riding shotgun in an alley cat's head.

Letmeoutofhere! she screamed soundlessly.

The figure in the alleyway called after her, its words still indecipherable. Nina's head spun—from the cold, from the unfamiliar motion of the cat, from the figure's voice that was shrill as shattering glass now. The cat bolted down Grasso Street, darting between the legs of pedestrians. Nina could feel whatever it was that was joining her to the cat letting go. It was like falling into an abyss, down and down, spinning in a tightening whirl until—

She blinked her eyes open to find Danny Connick's face close to hers, his hand on her shoulder as he shook her.

"Wha—?"

"Come on, dopey," he said. "The bus is here."

She sat up from her slouch on the bench, still disoriented. The bus loomed up behind Danny like some beached leviathan. The sounds of the street made a harsh, confusing dissonance that rang painfully in her head. She had an ache behind her eyes.

"Bus?" she said.

"Are you on drugs, Caraballo?" Danny asked.

"No, I . . ."

Had she just imagined it all? Fallen asleep for real here on the bench like some dippy bag lady?

She glanced back at the mouth of the alleyway. Did she still feel a chill wind coming from it? Were those eyes she saw in its depths—eyes still watching her—or just splashes of graffiti glinting from an errant ray of morning sun?

The bus driver honked his horn.

"Are you kids coming or what?" he shouted down at them.

Danny hauled her to her feet and aimed her up the steps to the door of the bus. He showed his pass, dug in Nina's pocket until he came up with hers, then walked her down to a seat in the back. Nina was vaguely aware of everybody watching her, but she still felt too out of it to be embarrassed by all the unwanted attention.

"Don't you know what dope can do to you?" Danny hissed in her ear when they were sitting down. "Would you look at the mess you are—and it's not even nine o'clock. I always thought you were more together than this, Nina."

"I . . . I'm not on drugs," Nina replied.

"Then what's the matter with you?"

Nina shrugged.

You wouldn't believe me if I told you, she thought. And then she realized that she was sharing a seat with him and was going to be stuck doing so all the way to school. Wonderful. She just hoped nobody she knew would see. If word got out, she'd just die.

"Well, you had me worried," Danny said.

Nina turned to look at him—really look at him—and suddenly felt awful. He was still a nerd, but here he was, after her snubbing him day in and day out for longer than she could remember, helping her out. Being nice. And all she could think of was how embarrassing it would be if anyone saw her with him.

Oh, that's being real gracious, Nina, she told herself.

"I guess I'm not quite over the flu I had yesterday," she said.

"Maybe you should have stayed home another day."

"God, you sound like my mother."

"Thanks a *lot*."

Nina couldn't help but laugh at the face he pulled.

She found Judy in the girls' washroom just off the rotunda around which the remainder of Redding High was built like

17

spokes emanating from the hub of a wheel. The room was full of cigarette smoke and gossip as the girls squeezed out their last few moments of freedom before homeroom. Judy was leaning close to a mirror, putting on the makeup that her parents wouldn't let her leave the house wearing, and grinned at Nina as she came in. She'd already changed from the prissy blouse and skirt her mother had bought her into a pair of faded jeans with a vintage flowered frock overtop.

Conversation bounced around the room all around them.

"Did you hear about Valerie and Brad?"

"Yeah, they broke up last night."

"He's so hot."

"Exceptional."

"She's got to be dippy to break up with him."

"I heard that *he* dumped *her* because she was hanging out with Keith Larson."

"I think I'm getting a zit inside my nose."

"Oh, gross."

"Debbie's got 'em on her butt."

"Here's a flash. Beth Grant's quit school to dance at Pussy's."

"But that's a strip club."

"Tell me about it."

Nina let the conversation flow around her, waiting impatiently for Judy to be finished with her makeup.

"So how do I look?" Judy asked her finally.

"Totally cool," Nina assured her.

And it was true. Judy had skin so clear that Nina would kill for it, and her hair took to a perm like it was born curly. Nina had to spend ages every morning getting her own hair to hold more than a slight curl.

She waited until they were out in the hall on their way to homeroom before she told Judy what had happened to her that morning.

"That's just too weird," Judy said when she was done.

"Am I going crazy or what?" Nina wanted to know. "Danny thought I was on drugs."

Judy pulled a face at the mention of his name.

"What if it happens in class?" Nina said.

"You can't control it at all?"

Nina shook her head, but she was a little doubtful.

"I don't know," she said. "I'm always panicking so much, I don't really stop to think anything out. I just want *out* of whatever body I'm in."

"But . . ." Judy hesitated. "You *did* fall asleep waiting for the bus, didn't you?"

"I . . ."

Nina thought back, trying to place the morning's events in their exact order.

"I don't know," she said finally. "It feels like I only just closed my eyes for a second and then it all started to happen."

"Well, maybe—"

The bell rang, and there was a mad scurry in the hallway all around them—lockers slamming shut and kids rushing off to their homerooms.

"We'll talk later," Judy said as she and Nina joined the scramble not to be late.

ASH

Ash couldn't face going into school that Thursday morning. Since being canned for the weekend, she'd been on her best behavior for three days now, attending the endless round of boring classes, not missing one; getting home on time every evening to sit around in the bedroom she shared with Nina, where she had to put up with her cousin's sulky face studying her whenever she thought Ash wasn't looking; helping out around the house like the good little suck she was pretending to be.

But enough was enough. She had to steal at least the morning to herself or go nuts.

So she got up early and left the house before her cousin was even dressed. By the time Nina was walking to the bus stop with her mother, Ash had crossed town and claimed a bench in Fitzhenry Park. She sat there as the morning progressed, watching the last of the commuters trail into the office blocks that fronted the park, then enjoying the familiar sights of the park's regulars as they started their own day.

The cat lady was the first to arrive. She came pushing a battered grocery cart loaded with her life's belongings, and wrapped in so many layers of clothes that it seemed she carried her entire wardrobe on her back. From out of the cart she took a bag of dried cat food, which she fed to the cats that had congregated at the foot of the war memorial, drawn there by her crooning call of "Minoux, minoux," and the promise of food.

In rapid progression, others appeared: Pedro, the Hispanic storyteller who always arrived early to stake out the best spot by the fountain, from which he'd declaim his city fables to the noon crowds; a pair of buskers—a fiddler and a hammer dulcimer player, the latter of whom, Ash knew from previous experience, tended to spend more time tuning than playing; the bicycle man, his three-wheeler festooned with every accessory imaginable— lights and mirrors, flags and a transistor radio—with a baby stroller attached at the back, in which his dog, Surfer, sat, a thin, scraggly furred creature of indeterminate origin, wearing toy sunglasses. There were panhandlers, winos fresh from their free breakfast at the men's mission, other kids skipping school, banging about on their skateboards near the war memorial once the cat lady was gone, bleary-eyed junkies looking for their morning fix, women from the nearby barrio pushing their kids around in strollers or packing them on their shoulders as they stood around gossiping in groups, joggers, a couple of college-age kids throwing around a Frisbee, various fast-food and small goods vendors with their carts, and too many others to mention.

Ash sat and watched them go about their business, tapping the toes of her black boots against each other and keeping a careful eye out for the source of last night's unwelcome attention, but he, at least, didn't appear. She started to relax as the sun rode higher. The hammer dulcimer player finally got her instrument in tune and now she and the fiddler were playing the old Gerry and the Pacemakers' hit "Ferry Cross the Mersey," which sounded weird, but not too shabby, considering their odd choice of instrumentation for the piece.

Her mum used to like that tune. She had the original soundtrack to the film that was made from the song, and used to play the thing over and over again until Ash thought she'd go crazy if she heard it one more time.

She'd give anything to be back home with her mum, listening to it now.

A tight feeling grabbed her chest, and she could feel tears welling up in her eyes.

Let it go, she told herself. Just let it go.

But it was so hard. Three years was forever, but it still felt like only yesterday when Mrs. Christopher from next door was gently shaking her awake.

Oh, you poor child, I've terrible news. . . .

Ash rubbed at her eyes with a knuckle.

She was *not* going to sit here in public, crying like some baby. But there was an emptiness inside her, a hole that her mum had left behind when she died, which could never be filled. Ash was getting really good at hiding it, pretending it wasn't there—at least she was when she wasn't alone. But hearing that music now and remembering. . . .

The hole opened like the vast maw of some ancient monolithic beast and threatened to swallow her whole.

"Hey, girl. Gimme a kiss."

For a moment only the words registered—not the voice itself nor its humorous tone. Ash turned, anger flaring, only to fall away again.

"Oh, Cassie," she cried, and embraced the woman whose approach to her bench she'd never noticed.

Cassandra Washington was the closest thing Ash had to a best friend. In her late twenties and a street person by choice rather than need, Cassie had coffee-colored skin, wore her hair in a hundred tiny beaded braids, and was the prettiest woman Ash knew. She tended to dress flamboyantly. Today she was wearing a pair of tight red jeans tucked into orange hightops, a yellow blouse and a black matador's jacket and huge plastic hoop earrings and bracelets in a rainbow hue of day-glo colors. Plunked down at her feet was a bulging red canvas shoulder bag that held the tools of her trade: a complex puzzle of canvas and wood that folded out to become a small collapsible table and stool, a tablecloth hand-embroidered with ornate hermetic designs, a small brass change bowl and, wrapped in silk and boxed in teak, her tarot cards.

Cassie was a fortune-teller, and Ash hadn't seen her in months.

"I thought you'd gone out West," she said after they'd hugged.

"I did. And now I'm back."

"I'm glad."

Cassie gave her a considering look. "I can see that. You do

look like you need a friend, girl. You got yourself caught up in hard times again?"

"Same times as always," Ash said.

"Spinning the wheel and landing on empty?"

Ash nodded.

"Well, then," Cassie said, "why don't we head on over to Ernie's cart and buy us some tea, and then we'll see if we can't find some quiet place where we can talk about it?"

Ash poked Cassie's bag with the toe of her boot.

"What about your gig?" she asked.

"Oh, I don't need the money," Cassie assured her. "I've got me a squat in Upper Foxville these days and a juju man named Bones crashing there with me who just lives to keep me happy, so don't you worry none about me."

She stood up and shouldered her bag, then caught Ash's hand.

"C'mon, girl. We'll go do some serious tête-à-têting."

They bought their tea from Ernie's cart, Cassie loading hers with five spoons of sugar, which astonished Ash for a moment. She'd forgotten her friend's sweet tooth. But Ernie hadn't. The short, dark-complexioned Cuban pulled out a sticky bun, dripping with honey, from a bottom shelf of his cart and offered it to Cassie.

"We've got biscuits," Cassie said, patting her shoulder bag.

"For you," Ernie said, "on the house. To welcome you home."

Cassie laughed. "Well, when you put it like that. . . ."

Ernie was beaming at them as they wandered off.

Deeper in the park, centered around a series of statues depicting a satyr lipping a syrinx and three dancing dryads, was a small hilltop surrounded by cherry trees in full blossom. The area was called Silenus Gardens and had been funded by a rich Crowsea patron of the arts in honor of the poet Joshua Stanhold. The benches here were marble—the same stone as the statues— and the air was sweet with the heady scent of the blossoms.

"I love this place," Cassie said as she sat down on one of the benches. "When I'm here I feel like I'm hidden away from everything—not cut off, it's just that the world's sort of on hold." She smiled at Ash. "It's a good place to talk."

Ash nodded. "I like it, too. I come and sit here at night sometimes just to, I don't know . . . think, I guess."

"Did you know that nobody's ever been mugged or hurt in this part of Fitzhenry?" Cassie said. "There's magic places in the world, places where I figure whoever's in charge—God, Allah, a little gray accountant in a gray suit, a witchy earth momma, you take your pick—decided that there was only going to be good vibes and this is one of them.

"It's hard to find that kind of space in a big city. Most places, if they've got anything at all, have only got one. We're pretty lucky here. This city's got two."

"Where's the other one?" Ash asked.

"An old house in Lower Crowsea—I'll point it out to you sometime."

Cassie pried the lid off her tea container, broke a small pie-shaped wedge from it, then replaced it on the top of her Styrofoam cup.

"People should carry around their own cups so that vendors wouldn't have to use this kind of crap," she said, regarding the Styrofoam with a critical eye. "Plays hell with the environment."

Ash nodded.

"So why don't you tell me what's got you burning blue?" Cassie said.

Ash picked at the lid of her own tea container, not saying anything for a while. She looked at the statues. They looked so carefree and happy. She wondered what it would be like to feel that way, to not always be carrying this chip on her shoulder.

Cassie gave her all the time she needed. She ate her sticky bun, making a goopy mess of her chin and fingers, drank some tea. She acted like they were on a picnic, like conversation wasn't necessary, maybe not even wanted, but when Ash finally began to talk about what was bothering her, she gave the younger girl all of her attention.

"It's never easy, losing your momma like that," she said when Ash was done. "But we've been through all this before."

Ash nodded "I know. I've got to let it go. But I just can't seem to do it."

"Not let it go," Cassie said. "You don't forget. You've got to

24

put it into perspective, that's all. What's happened has happened. You can't change that. But now you've got to go on."

"I suppose."

"That's what your momma would've wanted you to do."

Ash sighed. "But it's not just that. It's ... I don't know. I don't feel normal."

"Hate to break this to you, girl, but that's part of the curse of being your age. When I think of the weird head spaces I was in when I was sixteen...."

Cassie gave her a rueful grin.

"But I'm always angry," Ash said. "*Always.* It's not right. I know it's not right. I don't *want* to be this way, but I can't seem to do anything about. My aunt and uncle think I'm just going to grow out of it. The student adviser thinks I'm just trying to get attention—that I'm only pretending I've got problems so that I can goof off in class."

"You know what's what," Cassie said. "Nobody else can know it for you."

"But maybe I need, you know, serious help ... ?"

Cassie didn't say anything for a moment. As she looked across the garden, Ash studied her profile and wished she could be like her. Cassie never seemed to have problems.

"I don't like to lecture," Cassie said finally, "but you're asking, right?"

Ash nodded.

"The thing is, you're bringing this all down on yourself."

"What do you mean?"

"Well, if you think things are going to go wrong, then they usually will. It's all got to do with your attitude, girl. I know this sounds like teacher/parent bull, but it's God's own truth. You walk around with a negative attitude and you're just naturally going to bring trouble and hard times down on yourself. The more trouble you get into, the easier it is to believe that the whole world's out to get you."

"But how do you stop from feeling negative?"

Cassie shook her head. "That's the real question, isn't it, just? It's kinda hard to think about feeling good when everything feels bad."

Ash nodded.

"Maybe you could try helping somebody else—you know, do something good for someone who's having their own problems without expecting anything in return. Like visiting old folks in a nursing home. Or volunteering at the hospital, talking to sick kids. Stuff like that."

"They wouldn't want me, looking the way I do."

"I'm not saying you should change the way you look—that's part of who you are. You'd be surprised how many people will take the time to find out what's ticking in there behind the gear. But *you've* got to take the time as well. I'm betting you've got as many preconceptions about them as they do about you."

An angry retort came riding up Ash's throat, but she bit it back before she could give it life. Because Cassie was right. Ash slumped lower on the bench and stared down at her boots. Everything Cassie was saying made sense. She'd told herself as much about a million times. But that didn't help the way she felt.

"Why don't I do a reading for you?" Cassie said.

Ash looked up in surprise. Cassie'd never offered to do a reading before, and Ash had never asked. She'd just assumed that it wasn't something that Cassie did for friends.

"Now you've got to take it with a grain of salt," Cassie said. "All the cards do is tell you possibilities—strong possibilities, mind you, but still just possibilities. Nothing's carved in stone. This is more like looking into a mirror, except instead of showing you a reflection of your face, it reflects what's going on in here." Cassie tapped her chest. "You up for it?"

"Sure."

Ash looked expectantly at Cassie's shoulder bag with all its paraphernalia, but Cassie just took a tattered set of cards from the inside pocket of her matador's jacket. They were held together with an elastic band.

"Uh," Ash began.

Cassie smiled. "You're wondering why I'm not using the ones in here?" she asked, patting her shoulder bag.

Ash nodded.

"They're my pretties," Cassie said. "They're for show. People

put out the money, I give 'em a performance—fancy gear, lots of mystery, the kinds of things they expect."

"Preconceptions," Ash said.

"You got it. Most people figure that if they don't pay for it, then it's not worth anything. And if they *do* pay for it, then they want a show. So I've got the fancy cards for them, wrapped in silk, stored in a box. Real pretty. Surface pretty. But these"—Cassie tapped the tattered cards she'd taken from her pocket—"now these are magic."

She undid the elastic and pushed it onto her wrist, then shuffled through the cards.

"We need a Significator," she said.

Ash nodded. She had an Aquarian tarot at home and had done some reading on how the cards were used, but she'd never actually tried to do a reading. You weren't supposed to do them for yourself, and who did she have that she could do one for? Nina? That was a laugh. Her cousin seemed scared to death of Ash's metal records, never mind her small occult library.

"The Page of Pentacles," Cassie said. "I think this'll do. Black hair and dark eyes . . . the Queen's maybe too old, what do you think?"

Ash looked at the card that Cassie had laid on the bench between them and drew a sharp breath.

"That's . . ."

Cassie looked up with a grin. "You. Yeah."

"But it's *really* me."

The cards looked old—all tattered around the edges, the images worn almost threadbare in places. But the painting depicted on the card that Cassie had laid down looked exactly like Ash, right down to the skeleton earring and A in a circle Anarchy-symbol stud she wore in her left lobe, and the Motorhead patch on the pocket of her jean jacket. It was so perfectly her that it could have been a photograph.

"How . . . ?"

"Magic cards," Cassie said. "Don't worry about it, girl." She handed the rest of the pack over.

"But—"

"Give 'em a shuffle," Cassie prompted her.

For long moments, all Ash could do was stare at that image of herself that lay on the bench between them. The pack in her hands felt warm—warmer than she thought they should from sitting in Cassie's pocket, next to her chest. She was suddenly aware that she'd been thinking of this as a game, but now it was brought home to her that it was far more real than that.

And it scared her.

"We don't have to go on," Cassie said gently.

Ash lifted her gaze to meet Cassie's. This was her friend, she thought. No matter what happened, Cassie wouldn't let her get hurt. And if it helped . . .

"No," Ash said. "It's okay."

She shuffled the cards slowly, thinking about what was troubling her, then handed the pack back to Cassie.

"This is a good place," Cassie said. "Remember that. Something kind's watching over us here."

She drew a card from the pack and laid it on top of the Significator. An image of Nina looked up at Ash from its face.

"This represents the general atmosphere," Cassie said. "I'm going to lay out the cards first, and then we'll talk the whole thing through, okay?"

Ash could only nod. Seeing first a picture of herself, and now one of Nina, on these old cards had left her with a numb feeling.

Cassie laid a second card across it.

"And this represents the opposing forces," she said.

The second card showed an image of the stranger who'd followed Ash home last night.

Ash suppressed a shiver.

"This shows the foundation of the matter."

The third card was placed under the others. The picture on it was of an old woman. Her features were a wrinkled webwork of lines, drawn tightest around dark brown eyes that seemed ageless. She looked like a Native American, dressed in a soft, beaded doeskin dress with a fur mantle over her shoulders. Her hair was braided, the braids entwined with feathers, cowrie shells and more beads. She held a staff with feathered ornamentation at its head and wore a small moose-skin pouch at her hip, held there by leather thongs tied to a beaded belt.

29

Ash had never seen her before in her life. She'd also never seen that image before in any tarot deck. But before she could ask Cassie about it, her friend was already going on to the next card.

"This shows an influence that has recently passed away."

The fourth card went to the left of the Significator. On it was an odd mechanical image that seemed like a synthesis of machine and human-body parts. The colors were all shades of gray. It reminded Ash of a Giger painting or something from the movie *Aliens*.

"This shows the near future."

Laid above the Significator was a windswept, snowy plain with a tower rising from it. No, a tree. But it looked like a tower, with hundreds of small windows running up its face. Ash got a feeling of utter desolation from the image.

"This shows the far future."

The sixth card was placed to the right of the Significator, completing a cross shape. It carried the image of a wolf wearing a crown woven from a rosebush. The leaves on the branches were still green, and there was a red blossom in full bloom nestled in among the thorns above the animal's left ear.

"This shows your fears."

Cassie started a row of cards to the right of the cross the others formed with the seventh card. Depicted on it were the remains of a building ravaged by fire. Ash's pulse quickened when she realized it was the building in St. Ives where she and her mother had lived.

"This represents the influence of your family and friends."

The eighth card was laid above the seventh. On its picture, Ash's aunt and uncle stood in a summer glade. Their limbs were wrapped with the roots and boughs of the surrounding vegetation. Ash got a sense of both hope and menace from the image.

"This represents your own hopes."

The ninth card continued the row. It showed the back of a figure climbing to reach a summit. The figure was only a few feet from the top, but there were no more handholds. An arm came down from the top of the picture, reaching to help the climber. With only the limb in the picture, there was no way to tell who it was that was on the summit, reaching down.

That's me, Ash thought. But whose hand was that?

"And this shows the final outcome," Cassie said, drawing a final card from the pack.

She laid the last card above the ninth, completing the row of four cards that lay to the right of the cross that the first six had formed.

Ash looked at the card, then quickly lifted her gaze to Cassie's face. Her pulse was tapping out double-time like the frenzied riffing of a metalhead's guitar break.

"What . . . what does it mean?" she asked.

There was a look in Cassie's eyes that she'd never seen before. Cassie seemed to be drawn into herself, yet looking far away at the same time. It was like she was there, but not there. Here, but gone.

Ash's uneasiness deepened. Fears came skittering up her spine like they were carried on tiny rat's claws.

"Cassie?" Ash asked again when her friend didn't reply. "What's going on?"

"I . . . I don't know," Cassie said.

They both looked down at the final card again. It lay there, its face blank. No picture. No image. A clean slate.

The comforting feeling that had pervaded the garden when they'd first arrived seemed to be draining away, and there was a sudden chill in the air.

Cassie started to reach for the last card when a gust of wind arose from nowhere and scattered the reading onto the path by their feet. The cards lay on the pavement like so many haphazardly fallen leaves. Cassie sat there, her hand still outstretched to pick up the cards, her eyes looking off into unseen distances.

Nothing bad happens here, Ash told herself as she tried to stop from shivering.

But what if you brought something bad to this place? What if there was something wrong inside you and it got loose in here, taking the magic, twisting it? The way she had something wrong inside of her . . .

Cassie shook herself suddenly. The odd expression in her features smoothed away. Matter-of-factly, she bent down and retrieved the cards, returning them to the pack. She unrolled the rubber band from her wrist, placed it around the pack, then returned the pack to the inner pocket of her jacket.

"Cassie?" Ash said. "What's going on? Why was there nothing on that last card? *How* can there be pictures of me and Nina and everybody on those cards?"

"Like I told you," Cassie replied. "They're magic cards."

"Is something bad going to happen to me?"

"Not if I can help it."

That was far from comforting, Ash thought.

"What did the cards—"

"Nobody's going to hurt you," Cassie assured her. "You've got my word on that, and Cassie Washington doesn't jive. Okay?"

"But the reading . . . ?"

"I'm still working on it," Cassie said. "I've just got to think it through a bit more before I talk about it."

She stood up and shouldered her bag.

God, Ash thought. Cassie was taking off. She didn't know if she could handle that.

"I don't think I can be alone right now," she said.

"Who's leaving you? You're coming with me, girl."

"Where are we going?"

"To my squat. This is something I want to talk over with Bones."

At Ash's blank look, Cassie smiled.

"I told you, girl. He's a juju man, and that's what we've got working here. Juju—deep and thick. So what we need's a juju man to show us what it means."

Ash didn't know what was going on, but she trusted Cassie enough to let herself be led away, out of the park and on a northbound subway to Upper Foxville, where Cassie and Bones were sharing an abandoned building with a dozen or so other squatters.

Ash had never been in the part of Upper Foxville where Cassie and Bones were squatting. Their building was a couple of blocks north of Gracie Street, right in the heart of the square mile of empty buildings and rubble-strewn lots that were all that was left of the well-intentioned designs of a developers' consortium who'd planned to turn the area into an inner-city version of the 'burbs. Once the whole area had been just like the blocks south of Gracie—low-rent apartment buildings and tenements—but now it was home only to squatters, junkies, bikers, and the like.

It wasn't the kind of place that Ash would go into on her own. There were some places where it just wasn't worth hanging out, rep or no rep. Even walking through the rubble-strewn streets at Cassie's side, Ash felt nervous. She saw junkies congregated in the mouth of one alleyway, haunted eyes checking them out as they went by. The whistles and jeers of some street toughs followed them as they went by another. At a corner near Cassie's building, a lone biker with the colors of the Devil's Dragon emblazoned on the back of his dirty jean vest sat astride a chopped-down Harley and watched them from under hooded eyelids.

It was with relief that Ash followed Cassie into her squat to meet Bones.

The inside of the building was dressed up with graffiti—everything from spray-painted Anarchy symbols to crudely scrawled commentaries on various sexual perversions. Garbage and refuse littered the halls and stairwells. But on the second floor, the walls had been scrubbed down, the halls and rooms swept out.

"How're you doing?" Cassie asked her as they walked down a long empty hallway.

"Okay, I guess."

Ash thought about what had gone down in the Silenus Gardens earlier.

"But I'm still kind of shaken up," she admitted.

"Me, too," Cassie said.

Ash gave her a troubled look. It made her feel a little better to know that Cassie shared her fears. The problem was, though, that she was looking to Cassie to solve everything for her and if Cassie thought it was bad . . .

She didn't let herself continue that train of thought.

"Hang tough," Cassie told her. "We've got some high-powered help with Bones in our corner."

Bones was a Native American—a full-blooded Kickaha, a small local tribe that belonged to the Algonquian language family. He was older than Cassie, in his late twenties, which made him positively ancient as far as Ash was concerned. His skin had a dark coppery cast and his features were broad—nose flat, dark eyes set widely apart, square chin. He wore his long black hair in a single braid that was almost as long as the one Ash's aunt had, and dressed like a punker in faded black jeans, torn at the knees, scuffed work boots and a plain white T-shirt.

They found him in a back room on the second floor, sitting cross-legged in front of a small tepee of twigs. There were odd things woven in among the twigs. Small shells. Pigeon feathers. What looked like animal claws. Little strips of leather with animal fur still on them.

Bones wasn't anything like Ash had expected. He seemed as spaced as Cassie had been back at the park, gaze turned inward, but looking as though it was seeing into far, invisible distances at the same time. He gave no indication that he even knew they were there.

Great, Ash thought. We've come to get advice from a space cadet.

But as soon as Cassie and Ash sat down across from him, his dark eyes focused on them. For a moment, there was such a sense of power about him that it literally crackled in the air and made the small hairs on Ash's arms stand up as though charged with static. Then he gave them a toothy grin that transformed him into what Ash could only think of as a clown.

He pulled a plastic bag filled with jujubes from his pocket and popped a red and a black one in his mouth, chewing them with relish. Obviously he shared Cassie's sweet tooth. Ash just hoped that those candies weren't what Cassie had meant about his being a juju man.

"Hey, Cassie," he said. "The pickings poor?"

"I never even set up," she replied. "Ran into a friend, and she's got a problem."

The clownish features turned to her.

"Hey, Ash," he said. "Good to meet you." He offered her the bag of candies. "You want one?"

Ash shook her head. She glanced at Cassie.

"Uh, maybe my coming here wasn't such a good idea," she started, then paused to give Bones a closer look.

How had he known her name?

"I know what he looks like," Cassie said, speaking of Bones as though he wasn't present, "but trust me on this. He can't help acting the way he does. He's got too much of Nanabozho in his blood."

"Nana who?" Ash asked.

"You've got to laugh," Bones said. "If you don't laugh, you cry."

Cassie nodded. "Ain't that the truth."

Ash shook her head. There were things going on here, an underlying resonance that she just couldn't get a grip on.

"Here's the problem," Cassie said.

She launched into a description of what had happened in the park, taking Bones through the incomplete reading and how it had been interrupted. As she spoke of the images on the cards, each one rose up in Ash's mind's eye, as clearly as though the cards were still spread out in front of her. Ash started when Bones suddenly spoke to her.

"What did the images mean to you?" he asked.

The clown was gone—except for a vague and distant flicker of humor in the back of Bones's eyes. Ash was taken aback with his sudden seriousness. The images of the cards—so clear in her mind when Cassie had been describing them—tangled into a muddle.

"Ah . . . ," she began.

"We'll take them one at a time," Cassie said, helping Ash out. "The first one was of a girl your age."

Ash gave her a grateful look. "That was my cousin Nina."

With a little prompting from Cassie, Ash ran through the rest of them, explaining who the people were and how they related to her life. Some of the images she couldn't explain—the wolf with the crown of thorns, the old Native American woman; others she could only guess at—the burned ruin of the building that had housed the apartment she and her mother had shared in St. Ives, her aunt and uncle in the glade, their limbs tangled up with branches and roots.

When they'd gone through all ten cards, Bones nodded thoughtfully.

"I see," he said.

From the floor behind him, he picked up a small tanned hide pouch, which he set on his lap. Closing his eyes, he reached inside. Ash could hear a funny, muffled, rattling sound as he moved his hand around.

"What's he doing?" she asked Cassie.

Cassie put a finger to her lips.

Bones started to make a sound then.

"Ahhh, hyeh, hyeh-no, no-ya."

At first, Ash thought he was moaning, but then she realized it was a kind of droning chant. That sense of power she'd felt for just a moment, when she and Cassie had first sat down with him, returned—this time filling the room. Goose bumps went running up her forearms, and she couldn't quell a shivering that seemed to come from someplace deep inside her, right in the marrow of her bones.

The chanting grew louder.

"Ah-nya-hee, hey-no, hey-no."

With a sudden abrupt movement, Bones brought his hand out of the bag. Opening his hand, he scattered its contents on the floor between himself and the odd little tepee.

So that's where he got his name, Ash thought.

Tiny bones lay where they'd been strewn, forming a pattern that meant nothing to Ash—and probably nothing to Cassie as well, she thought—but obviously held meaning for Bones. He bent over them, fingers outstretched to follow the crazy-quilt pattern, hovering just a fraction above the tiny bones.

He was quiet now. The only sound in the room was that of their breathing. Ash studied the bones, trying to see what he saw in them.

What did they come from? she wondered. Birds? Mice? Maybe it was better not to know.

Bones scooped up the pattern, the motion as abrupt as the one that had initially cast it, and replaced the bones into their pouch.

"The trouble's not yours," he said once he'd put them away. "It touches you, but you're not its focus. Your pain and anger were the catalyst—calling the wraith from out of the spirit world—but once here, it found someone else to hunt."

Ash's pulse began to quicken again.

"What . . . what do you mean?" she asked.

"He means a spirit from the Otherworld was drawn to you by the strength of your emotions," Cassie explained.

"C'mon," Ash said. "Get real."

"Trouble is," Cassie went on, as though Ash hadn't interrupted, "it found somebody else to haunt."

Ash shook her head. "Just saying any of this is real, what makes that a bad thing? It's not my problem anymore, right?"

Cassie said nothing, but the recrimination was plain in her eyes. Bones merely lowered his gaze to that odd little tepee that sat on the floor between them.

Ash sighed. "Okay. I wasn't thinking. Or maybe I was just thinking of myself."

Bones gave her an encouraging smile.

"So what makes it harder if this"— she stumbled over the word, because she was stumbling over the whole concept of the thing—"spirit's chasing after someone else?"

She had her little occult library, and she liked to think about the stuff she read in those books, but deep down inside where it really counted, she'd never really accepted that any of it was real. Because if it was real, then her mother would have contacted her. That was the whole reason she'd gotten into exploring that kind of thing in the first place.

But her mother never did.

Because when you were dead, you were dead for good. You couldn't feel anything anymore. You were gone. It didn't matter to you anymore.

But it wasn't the same for those left behind. . . .

"If the spirit wanted you," Bones said, "we could call her up right now and deal with the matter. As it is, we've got to track down who it wants and then convince that person—first, that the problem's real, and second, that we can help."

"My money's on her cousin," Cassie said.

Ash shook her head. "Nina? No way. She's about as interested in this kind of thing as I am in her goofy friends."

"The hunter chooses," Bones said. "Not the victim."

Maybe so, Ash thought, but Nina? Who'd want *her*?

"What about this guy that followed me from the occult shop last night?" she asked. "I'd think he was a better candidate."

"He bothers me," Cassie said.

Bones nodded. "He doesn't fit in. And I don't believe in coincidence. But the spirit is a feminine aspect—the bones tell me that, as did the foundation card of your reading—and traditionally, for this kind of a hunt, she would be seeking one of her own sex."

"Why's that?" Ash wanted to know.

"It appears that we're dealing with one of Grandmother Toad's little manitou cousins."

"But she's always been a helper," Cassie said, frowning.

Bones nodded. "True enough. But the manitou are amoral. This one appears to be withering; she seeks the energy of a young female spirit to replenish the loss of her own."

"You mean like a vampire?" Ash asked.

She couldn't help but laugh. The idea was ridiculous. Some Indian bloodsucker going after her cousin? Yeah, right.

"Something like that," Bones said, his features solemn.

Everything tightened up inside Ash. Jeez. He sounded like he really meant it.

She cleared her throat. "So . . . uh, what do we do about it?"

"I have to meet your cousin," Bones said.

Like Nina'd come traipsing into Upper Foxville on Ash's say-so. Or maybe she could have Cassie and Bones over for dinner? What would her aunt and uncle have to say about that?

The loose train of her thoughts skidded to a halt.

Nina's parents.

"She's part Indian," Ash said. "My cousin Nina. Her dad's half something or other."

And come to think of it, Nina's parents would probably welcome Cassie and Bones into their house without blinking an eye. It wasn't like they were exactly yuppies or anything themselves. Not with their old psychedelic Fillmore posters still hanging on the wall, twenty years down the road from when the gigs were first being advertised. The Grateful Dead. The Acid Test Band. Big Brother and the Holding Company.

"Is she now," Bones said.

Ash nodded. "I don't know what tribe her grandmother was

from, but her dad's lived around here all his life, so maybe it's some local one."

"I think you guessed right," Bones said to Cassie. "We'll have to—"

He paused as a sudden clamor arose from downstairs in the building.

"Oh, crap," Cassie said.

"What's the matter?" Ash asked.

Cassie sighed. "The cops are running one of their little sweeps through the squats."

"The cops? What for?"

"The consortium that owns these blocks has convinced some member of the city council to get the police department to occasionally pick up and disperse the transients from the area."

She sounded as though she was quoting a newspaper article.

"But that's not fair. Nobody else is using the buildings, so why can't you?"

"Because if something happened to someone in one of them and they decided to sue, the developers would be held legally responsible. And since you can bet that they don't have any insurance on these places . . ."

Ash started to get up. "Well, let's get out of here. The last thing I need is for my aunt and uncle to have to bail me out of juvie hall."

Cassie laid a hand on Ash's knee, preventing her from rising.

"Cassie. I'll get grounded for *months*."

"Don't be scared," Cassie said. "But there's only one way we can get out of here without them catching us."

Ash could hear the brusque voices of policemen on the ground floor as they rousted the squatters they found in there. The sound of arguments came down the hall. Something that sounded like a door getting kicked in.

"What are you talking about?" Ash said.

Cassie merely looked at her companion. "Bones?"

He was already chanting—a different chant this time.

"Oh-na, oh-nya-na, hey-canta, no-wa-canta . . ."

He'd produced a pipe from somewhere. It had a long stem. From the bowl hung leather thongs strung with beads, shells and feathers. He stuffed the bowl with dark tobacco leaves.

Ash could hear the police coming up the stairwell.

"Cassie," she began.

She tried to rise again, but Cassie's grip tightened painfully on her leg, making it impossible for her to get up.

"I'm sorry, Ash," Cassie said. "But it's best you come with us."

"But you're not moving!"

Bones broke off his chant and lit the pipe. Thick smoke clouded the air—more smoke than Ash knew could possibly have come from such a little pipe in so little time. She felt a sudden sense of vertigo, like she was dropping too fast in an elevator. Her stomach lurched queasily. She couldn't see anything in the room anymore—just the acrid smoke that stung her eyes and made her cough. She could feel Cassie's hand, still on her knee, but no longer holding her so tight. But underneath her, where the floor had been—

Panic came skittering up her spine.

Oh, jeez.

The hardwood was gone and she could feel a rough, uneven surface of some kind of stone. A wind arose, tossing her hair, tattering the smoke and dispersing it.

Ash's panic turned to numb disbelief as she realized that the three of them were now sitting on top of a huge granite outcrop, high above acres of forestland. The treetops were a green sea that spread off into the horizon for as far as she could see.

"C-C-Cassie . . . ?" Ash mumbled, finding the words hard to shape, her throat was so dry. "Where . . . where are we . . . ?"

"The spirit world," Bones replied.

She looked at him. That mad clown humor danced in his eyes, but Ash didn't think there was anything funny about him anymore. He was a real, honest-to-God shaman. A guy who could do that—he could do anything, couldn't he? So what was he doing, hiding out in a squat in Upper Foxville?

What did he want with *her*?

"Don't be afraid," Cassie said again, her voice pitched soothingly.

She wasn't afraid, Ash wanted to tell her. She was terrified. But her throat had closed right up on her, and all she could do was stare around her, willing herself to wake up from what had to be a dream.

NINA

After school, Nina pulled one of the old-fashioned wicker chairs from behind her parent's house. She positioned it in the middle of the postage stamp that served as a backyard, where it would catch the last of the afternoon sun. Changing into a pair of baggy shorts and a blouse that tied loosely closed across her stomach, she brought a lemonade and the latest issue of *Sassy* out to the chair, and sat down with her glass balanced on one fat arm of the chair, the magazine on the other.

She wasn't in the world's greatest mood.

First, Judy had used her as an excuse to head over to the mall with Bernie Fine. Nina didn't mind covering for her friend, but she'd really wanted a better talk with Judy than the one they'd managed to squeeze in at lunch time. That was the trouble with boys. They interfered with the serious business of a real friendship.

Then Nina had to listen to her mother railing about how the school had phoned her while she was at the studio because Ashley had skipped again, and did Nina know where her cousin was, and just wait until she got her hands on that girl, because enough was enough. Take it out on Ashley, Nina had wanted to tell her mother. But of course Ashley wasn't here, so Nina had to listen to it all. It'd serve Ashley right if she got canned for a year.

But the real problem Nina had was her dreams. It was bad enough having them once a week or so for the past year. Now they were intruding on her waking life, and *that* she didn't need at all. Next thing she knew, she'd space out in the middle of volleyball practice and start barking like a dog or something, and wouldn't that be great? She got enough flak because half the school thought she was a nerd; the other half didn't know or care that she existed.

She didn't know what their problem was. If you had to go to school, you might as well do the best you could. Besides, a lot of the classes—History, English, but especially the Maths and Sciences—were really *interesting*. It wasn't like she didn't fool around some, skipping the odd class, hanging out in the washroom. But that wasn't enough for some people. If you wanted to be truly cool, you weren't supposed to get good grades either.

Nina sighed. None of which helped her with her current problem.

She considered the advice that Judy had left her with before she and Bernie had gone off to the Williamson Street Mall. Judy said that instead of panicking, next time Nina should try to get into being whatever kind of animal she was dreaming she was.

"Like in *Caddyshack*," she told Nina. "Remember? When Chevy Chase is explaining the zen of golf?"

"*Be* the ball," Nina said before Judy could declaim what she thought was the second best line in the film, the first being Dangerfield's comment on his own fart: "Did somebody step on a duck?"

Caddyshack was one of Judy's favorite movies because two of her heroes—Bill Murray and Chevy Chase—were both in it.

"They're too old," Nina complained more than once when they got into a discussion about it.

"But they're funny."

"Sometimes."

The reruns of "Saturday Night Live" with them in it were sure funnier than the current crop. But, be the ball? Be the animal? Don't panic?

Sure. Like she could just turn her fears on and off.

Nina sighed again. I'm beginning to sound like an old lady, she thought, and turned to her magazine.

Her mum used to complain about her reading teen magazines because of "the kind of role models they presented to impressionable young minds," never mind Nina's arguments that their fashion and make-up spreads were the best way to keep on top of what was hot. But she didn't mind *Sassy* after Nina pointed out that it also carried articles like the current issue's "Who Wants to Change the World?" which dealt with sexism, animal rights, nuclear disarmament, and the like.

Nina flipped through the pages, agreeing with one writer that the lead singer from INXS should never have cut his hair and wondering how the models kept their complexions so clear, but all the time thinking about her dreams. When she got to the Help column—in one letter someone wanted to know how to tell when a guy was using you, another wanted to know what orgasm meant—she thought maybe she should write in with her problem.

She knew what the reply would be: Go see a shrink.

At least it would be if they were honest.

She closed the magazine. It was no use. She couldn't get the dreams out of her head—particularly the one she'd had at the bus stop this morning. Just thinking of that weird figure standing in the alleyway made her shiver.

After awhile, she got up and went inside. Writing up a Biology lab helped take her mind from things until dinner, when things got horrible because her parents were both mad and worried about Ashley's disappearance.

Good riddance, was Nina's only comment on the subject, but she knew enough to keep it to herself.

After dinner she called Judy, but all Judy wanted to do was talk about Bernie. Bernie did this and said that. He'd asked Judy to a movie this weekend, and did Nina think she could cover for her? It was only going to be their second date, but it was sort of like going steady, wasn't it?

Nina listened for a while, getting off the phone as soon as she could with the excuse of having to do the homework she'd already finished. Instead she just went to bed.

At least I'll be safe from dreams for awhile, she thought as she lay under the covers, staring up at the ceiling.

They rarely came more than once a week. This week she'd already had two.

She drifted off, wondering what had happened to Ashley in a sleepy, half-interested fashion—

—and woke to find her skin covered with fur.

She was starting to get used to it. Not that she liked it—no way, absolutely not—but she was getting to the point where the first thing she did was run a quick check on herself to see what kind of animal she was dreaming she was. The panic always came later. When she tried to move. When she *had* to move because something awful was about to happen if she didn't. . . .

This time she was a wolf.

It wasn't fair. This was the third time in two days. But she'd been a dog before—a mangy little street mutt that only stood about as tall as a big cat—and was almost getting the hang of moving its body when a big German shepherd thought that she'd make a nice meal. A wolf's body wasn't that different, so maybe she could get it to work for her.

Be the ball.

She moved one paw tentatively, then another, concentrating for all she was worth until she'd taken a few wobbly steps, her tail stuck straight out behind her for balance. She grinned as she shuffled forward a few more steps and came face to face with a sharp drop. A steep cement ravine lay in front of her. Beyond it was a low wall. Beyond it, the wolf's keen night vision brought her a view of the broad sweeping acres of the Metro Zoo.

She knew a moment's frustration. Here she was, in the body of a pretty heavy-duty predator—I mean, who was going to mess around with a wolf?—and she couldn't go off exploring in the body. But then she realized that she was also safe from outside threats as well. No big brave hunter was going to be taking pot shots at her with his rifle. She didn't have to worry about hiding out anywhere, because where could she be safer than locked up here at the Zoo? It was the perfect opportunity to learn more about the animal and what she was doing in its body.

Be the ball.

Maybe she should do her next biology paper on wolves.

She took a few more exploratory steps, her confidence rising as she started to get the hang of moving around on four legs. The

wolf's olfactory senses brought a staggering world of exotic odors to her nostrils. She sifted through the myriad scents, enjoying the challenge of puzzling them all out.

At the far side of the wolves' enclosure, something moved.

A tiny gibber of fear went scurrying up Nina's spine, but then she saw that it was just more of the Zoo's small pack. A half-dozen wolves were moving out of the deeper shadows, padding towards her. The alpha pair—the pack leaders—were in the fore, the other wolves deferring to them.

Hi there, Nina wanted to say.

Her words came out in a rolling growl, startling her.

I sound like something out of a werewolf movie, she thought.

She started to grin at the notion, but stopped when she realized that her growl had woken an adverse reaction in the other wolves.

Oh, jeez, Nina thought. What did I say in wolf-talk?

The alpha male approached her on stiff legs, an answering growl rumbling from deep in his own chest.

Easy, boy, she tried to say. I didn't mean anything bad.

The words just came out as more growls. The hackles on the alpha male's neck stood at attention. He paced closer, the other members of the pack circling around her.

Nina began to remember things she'd read about wolves. Like how closely knit a pack was and how they'd drive outsiders away from their territory. She was in the body of one of their companions, but she was probably acting wrong. Probably smelled wrong.

She shot a quick glance at the enclosing gulch. It was too steep for her to dare the drop. But if she couldn't get away—if the wolves couldn't drive her off from what they considered their "territory"—what would they do?

The answer came with an abrupt attack from the alpha male.

He lunged at her, teeth, snapping at her shoulder. She flailed out of his way as soon as he moved, so that while his teeth caught at her flesh, they just nipped her shoulder, not breaking the skin. But the pain was still intense—a hot fire burning in her shoulder muscles—and the panic she'd been so successfully keeping at bay now came clawing up her nerve ends.

She fell onto her side from the sudden motion of evading the wolf's attack, scrabbling immediately to her feet and backing away. But then she had the drop at her back, the pack in front of her.

Wake up, she told herself. Wakeupwakewup*wakeup*!

But nothing changed.

Except that the alpha male lunged at her again.

ASH

"It's okay," Cassie said. "We're not going to be here long."

She gave Ash an easy smile, like they were still just hanging around in the Silenus Gardens instead of off in some Neverneverland. Incongruous though that smile was in this place, in this situation, it was still far more reassuring than the mad, lopsided grin that pulled at Bones's features.

"Right," Ash said in a small voice. "Not long."

She still couldn't believe the "here" part. Where had Upper Foxville gone? And *how* had they left it? From the craggy granite outcrop on which the three of them were sitting, all she could see was virgin wilderness. Thousands and thousands of acres of wild forestland, stretching all the way to the distant horizon, broken only by the odd islanding outcrop like the one they were on— ancient stone bones, pushing their way up through the forest to reach for the sky.

This place looked like it had never known the step of a white man, little say a block of tumbled-down tenements.

"It's not good to stay in this place for too long," Bones said, a solemn look taking the place of his grin. But laughter continued to bubble in the back of his eyes.

Ash gave him a quick glance, then looked away across the panorama of forestland. She knew he was Cassie's friend, so she should be able to trust him, but something about him gave her the willies. It wasn't so much him, she realized, as what he could do. Like whip them all away from reality with nothing but a chant and some dry ice effects that would do Motorhead proud.

Although maybe they hadn't been whipped away. The smoke that had come from his pipe ... maybe it was just some kind of drug and they were all *imagining* that they were in this place. Right now the cops could be hauling their bodies off, while they sat around just spacing out. Wonderful.

Except it felt too real for that. Ash wasn't sure if that made her feel relieved or not. She was so unsettled about the whole thing that it was hard to tell what she felt.

She looked back at him finally.

"Why not?" she asked. "What would happen if we stayed here for too long?"

"This is the spirit world," he replied, "where the manitou live. We're not meant to visit it for long periods of time in our corporeal forms. It's a place our spirits travel to when we seek knowledge or wisdom or to speak with the shades of our ancestors, but our bodies create ripples of dissonance the longer they remain, changing them, changing the land. Those changes aren't always healthy."

"What do you mean by speaking with your ancestors?" Ash wanted to know.

"Ghosts sometimes walk this land before they are reborn or travel on."

"Do you know how to call them up?"

"I have spoken to the voices of the past," Bones said.

"But it's not a good idea," Cassie said.

Bones nodded. "The dead don't often remember the details of their past lives. If you call them up, they rarely recognize you. Like manitou, they can play tricks on you—not intentionally, not for the prank itself as a manitou might, but simply because you were foolish enough to call them up in the first place. Everything has its price—especially in this realm—and sometime the coin is dear."

"Too dear," Cassie added. "You can come away crazy."

"And sometimes you don't come away at all," Bones said.

But her mother would recognize her, Ash thought. How could she not?

"Because this is a land of the spirit—of the mind," Bones went on, "it's difficult to trust one's perceptions here, particularly when viewing it through the coarse senses of the body. Time travels in paths, like a gust of wind. On one path, it travels at the same speed as it does in the world we have so recently quit. Along another, one minute can be a week. Or a week can be a day."

"Like Faerie," Ash said, having read about mortals straying for a night into Faerie, only to find that seven years had passed when they returned.

"This *is* that same Faerie," Cassie said. "It's the otherworld where the spirits live. You can call them manitou or elves or *loa*—doesn't much matter. Each of us sees them differently. We see the land differently. But it's always the same place."

"But—"

"Time we were going," Bones said, rising fluidly to his feet. "We've been here long enough as it is."

"Going?" Ash asked, scrambling to her own feet. "Can't you just enchant us back?"

Bones nodded. "But if I do that from here, we'll end up back in the squat with the police. We're just going to move on a bit and put some distance between us. Think of this visit as a short-cut to get from one place to another—without being seen by anyone in our world."

Ash looked around herself, struck not so much by what Bones had said as by what he hadn't said.

"There's people watching us here?" she asked.

She didn't see a sign of life.

"Spirits watch us," Bones told her with that mad humor rising in his eyes again. "Come along now and stay close. It's easier to get lost here than you might think."

Spirits were watching? Ash thought. Maybe her mother was in there behind the trees, looking out at her. . . .

"Come on," Cassie said.

Bemused, Ash nodded and followed the pair as they made their way down into the trees on the one side of the steep hill that was more easily negotiable than the others. She peered in among the trees as they went, pausing each time she thought she saw something move, but it was always just the way the light caught a branch, or her own shadow cast in among the cedar and firs.

"Don't lag," Cassie told her after she and Bones had to pause for the fourth time to let her catch up. "You don't want to get lost in this place. Trust me."

"I won't get lost," Ash assured her.

Cassie nodded. She and Bones moved on, Ash following. But then she saw something else move and had to stand very still, trying to make out what it was. This time it wasn't either her own shadow or sunlight on a branch. This time there really was someone in there, looking back at her. She could make out a vague glimpse of dark hair under a gossamer veil that fell from an odd headpiece, something along the lines of those she'd seen in medieval paintings. The body was cloaked in black—a long dress or a cloak. From its shape, Ash could tell that this was definitely a woman.

"Who are you?" she asked softly.

Cassie and Bones had paused again, waiting for her.

"Ash!" Cassie called.

"Just a sec," Ash replied.

She took a step closer to where the mysterious figure was standing. She had a momentary sensation of the ground shifting underfoot—a smaller version of the vertigo that she'd experienced when Bones had brought them to this place from the squat in Upper Foxville—and then everything changed.

Gone were the cedars and pines. Gone was the daylight. Twilight lay thick in the woods now—the trees predominantly birch, rather than the cedar and firs they'd been only a moment ago. The sloping ground had leveled out, making Ash stumble for balance.

She looked back the way she'd come—she'd only taken one step, but she might as well have stepped halfway across the world. And maybe she had, because this no longer felt like a North American forest. Instead it had an Old World feel to it, like the forests back home in England. The boughs of fat beech and oak, wych elm and silver birch trees spread a thick canopy above. Below them, the ground was deep with old mulch and cleared of much of its undergrowth.

And Cassie and Bones were gone.

The only trace of them she could find was the sound of their voices. They had a distant, far-off quality to them—as though they came drifting to Ash from the other side of a hill. Or were seeping in through some muffling barrier. Cassie's voice, calling her name. And then Bones, talking.

"It's too late," he was saying. "She's gone where we can't follow."

"We *have* to find her," Cassie replied. "I'm responsible for her being here. I can't just go off and leave her in this place. She came to me for help and now look what I've done. If I don't find her, I won't be able to live with myself."

"You've no choice. There are a thousand thousand paths she might have taken. She might have stepped into yesterday. Or tomorrow. She might be in a time that never was, or never will be. We can't possibly follow. We could spend lifetimes looking for her and never even come close to finding her."

Ash shook her head. What was he saying? What did he mean?

Cassie was still arguing, but her voice was floating in and out of audibility, like a radio station's fluctuating signal, and Ash couldn't make out what she was saying. But she heard Bones.

"All we can do is go back and wait. And hope that she can find her way home."

Cassie said something else that Ash couldn't make out.

"We can pray," she heard Bones reply before his voice faded as well.

Ash stared at where she thought the sounds had been coming from.

Now I've done it, she thought.

Nervous fears went skittering up her spine. She started to take a step back, but then paused to take another look at the mysterious figure that had seduced her from the path she'd been following. She half-expected the woman to be gone, but she was sitting now on a rounded elm stump, short hazel bushes rising up behind her. She was looking at Ash with a faint smile that reminded Ash uncomfortably of Bones's mad humor.

The woman's veil fell only to the bridge of her nose in the

front, hiding her eyes, while it cascaded down to her ankles in back. The headpiece from which it hung seemed to be made of stiff leather, encrusted with small gems. Another gem—a blue stone in a gold setting—dangled like a pendant from a black choker and lay in the hollow of her throat. Her skin was pale, pale. In her hand she held a pomegranate, curiously bound with iconic silver bands.

She was heart-stoppingly beautiful, just as Ash remembered her mother had been.

She could hear Cassie's voice in her mind.

You can call them manitou or elves or loa—*doesn't much matter.*

But this woman wasn't her mum.

Each of us sees them differently.

She was like the fairy princesses in the stories that he mum used to read her.

We see the land differently.

Just like this forest was like a forest from back home.

But it's always the same place.

It felt familiar. Just as the woman seemed familiar.

Oddly enough, Ash's fears had washed away. The fact that she was lost in this forest didn't seem that important anymore. Nor did the fact that there was something dangerously alluring about this woman.

Trust me, everything about her said.

Except for her smile.

If you dare, was its message.

Ash took another step forward, and it was then that she noticed the birds. A raven sat on the elm stump beside the woman, its head resting on her lap beside the pomegranate. A hawk or a falcon was perched on a low-hanging branch her other side.

Magic, Ash thought. A magic bird lady in a magic place.

A faint voice cried out a warning in the back of her head. Cassie's voice.

You can come away crazy.

Maybe she already was crazy, because this whole afternoon had an insane feel about it.

And sometimes you don't come away at all.

So what was there to come back to? Just hassles and loneliness and that awful feeling of anger that constantly rode inside her.

She didn't feel angry here.

All she felt was a sense of wonder.

She moved closer still. The woman lifted her head. Through her veil, her eyes glittered, but their elusive expression remained hidden behind the gauze.

"Who are you?" Ash asked again.

"Let me show you something," the woman said, ignoring Ash's question.

Her voice was husky, but its tones were rimmed with a faint bell-like sound. She set aside the silver-banded pomegranate and pulled back the right sleeve of her dress to reveal a bracelet cluttered with dozens of silver charms. The charms jingled in a musical harmony to her voice as she deftly removed one. It lay for a moment in the palm of her hand—a miniature reproduction of some stoneworks, Ash saw, a circle of standing stones shrunk down into a tiny silver charm—then the woman tossed it onto the ground between them.

The raven cawed and raised its head from her lap. The other bird half-opened its wings, feathers rustling. Ash, for her part, could only stand there and stare around herself in open-mouthed wonderment as the charm grew, pushing back the forest until she and the mysterious woman were in the center of a circle of old worn standing stones.

"Nothing need be as it seems in this place," the woman said. "Only as you perceive it—as you need it to be."

She made an odd movement with her fingers and the stoneworks shrank down, the forest closing in around them once more, thicker and darker than before. The woman bent down and retrieved the charm, which she then refastened to her bracelet. When she straightened up, the hidden gaze behind her veil studied Ash again.

"Do you understand?' she asked.

Ash slowly shook her head.

"Who *are* you?" was all she could say.

"You can call me Lusewen."

The woman smiled, that same maddening smile, at Ash's bewildered expression.

"But a name's not enough, is it?" the woman went on. "You want my whole pedigree and history wrapped up and labeled, and then handed to you so that you can comfortably file me away in the proper slot in your mind. For all your 'open-mindedness,' you're really just as bad as your sister."

"I don't have a sister," Ash said.

"Not in the strictest sense of the word, perhaps, but your mothers were twins, weren't they? They shared the same genes. Surely that makes the two of you close enough almost to be sisters?"

"How do you know anything about me—about my family?"

How do you know nothing about me?" Lusewen responded.

"I only just met you. How could I know *anything* about you?"

The sense of wonder was fading, the ever-present anger rising up to push it aside.

"Temper, temper," Lusewen said.

Ash wanted to lash out at the infuriating woman, but caught herself just in time.

She's magic, she warned herself. Stay cool, because if you don't, she'll probably turn you into a frog.

"Where did you meet my sister?" she asked instead.

"I've never met her," Lusewen said. "I've only watched her spirit go totem-seeking. She's an unusual girl. There are always mysteries following her around."

"Mysteries?"

"Spirits."

"Like you?"

Lusewen smiled. "Still trying to fit me into a slot?"

"You're the one who said I was doing that," Ash replied. "I never did."

"But it's what you do. I know."

"I. . . ."

But then Ash thought about it. It was true that she tried not to make value judgments of people just by their appearance, but that didn't stop her from putting people into convenient little compartments in her mind. Punkers and straights, headbangers and preppies. You hung around with some, others you ignored, still others you avoided....

"What do you mean by totem seeking?" she asked to change the subject.

"Your sister's spirit is drawn out of her body into the bodies of animals, as though seeking the totemic influence that will guide her life."

"Nina?" Ash asked, the disbelief clear in her voice. "You've got to be kidding."

Lusewen stood abruptly and caught Ash's hand.

"Look," she said.

Again the forest dissolved, only this time it was replaced with something familiar. Lusewen had brought her to the Metro Zoo, right smack dab in the middle of the wolves' enclosure. Their appearance interrupted what seemed to be a confrontation between one of the wolves and the rest of the pack.

The pack scattered as she and Lusewen emerged from the spirit world into their midst. The wolves fled to other parts of the enclosure—all except the one that they'd been picking on. That one cowered near the lip of the concrete ravine that kept the wolves in their enclosure and was staring at them with—nervousness, yes, Ash realized, but there was exceptional intelligence present in the animal's eyes as well.

It had human eyes.

Her heartbeat did a sudden skidding double-time jig.

She'd recognize those eyes anywhere. They were Nina's eyes. It was Nina in that wolf's body....

Or at least it had been Nina. The wolf shivered violently, blinked, and then there was just an animal's mind behind its gaze. The wolf growled, baring its fangs, then fled as its companions had earlier.

But that had definitely been Nina in there.

The zoo faded as Lusewen returned them to the forest in the Otherworld. Ash felt a little weak-kneed and sat down right where she was standing.

How could the whole world change in the space of one afternoon? Ten hours ago, magic was something she read about in books about the occult, wishing it was real, but knowing deep down inside that it wasn't. Now she was in the middle of this spirit world—brought here by a shaman who was also an Upper Foxville squatter—talking to some wizard woman, finding out that her sweet little cousin was actually into some heavy-duty magic stuff all on her own. . . .

"Jeez," she said.

"Do you believe me now?" Lusewen asked.

Ash slowly nodded. "Kind of hard not to when it's all staring me right in the face. I never knew Nina had it in her."

"Oh, it's not her doing," Lusewen said. "As far as she's concerned, it's all a nightmare. A recurring nightmare where she finds herself inhabiting the bodies of animals and she doesn't understand why."

"Well, why *is* it happening?" Ash asked.

And why wasn't it happening to *her* instead, because she'd at least appreciate it.

Lusewen only shrugged in response, but then Ash remembered the reading that Bones had done for her earlier—the scatter of animal bones in his Foxville squat that had been cast to make sense of Cassie's Tarot reading.

The trouble's not yours, he had told her. *It touches you, but you're not its focus.*

The mixed-up stew of her emotions had drawn something out of the spirit world—out of *this* place—and then—

It found someone else to hunt.

It found Nina. And—she closed her eyes, trying to recall what it was Bones had said before she'd started joking to him about vampires. Something about a spirit getting weak—no, withering was the word he'd used. It was looking for the energy of a young female spirit to replenish the loss of her own.

Ash opened her eyes and regarded Lusewen with sudden suspicion.

Was she going to find a more likely candidate as to who that hunting spirit might be than the woman sitting right there in front of her?

"What's the deal?" she asked Lusewen. "What do you want from me?"

Lusewen gave her that maddening smile.

"I didn't come looking for you," she said. "You came—"

"Yeah, yeah. I stumbled on you. Except it was just an accident."

"In the spirit world, there is no such thing as coincidence."

"You're driving me crazy!" Ash cried.

Lusewen shook her head. "It's this place that's mad," she said. "Remember what I told you, nothing need be as it seems in this place. It's only as you perceive it—as you need it to be."

"I need help," Ash said.

"That's what I'm here for."

Ash's eyes narrowed. She studied Lusewen's features again, but though the woman still had that look about her that reminded Ash of Bones, Lusewen didn't seem to be mocking her. And why did she still look familiar? There was something about her—like a name that sat on the tip of your tongue but you just couldn't call it up.

Nothing need be as it seems to be in this place.

Right. So where did that leave her?

It's only as you perceive it—as you need it to be.

Was Lusewen even real? Had she just called the woman up from her own imagination?

"Can you send me home?" Ash asked.

Lusewen nodded. "But what about your sister?"

"She's not my—" Ash began, then she sighed.

Well, maybe in some ways she was. Or maybe she should start treating Nina like she was.

"What about her?" she asked.

"If you want to help her, you have to do it from here."

"And what do I have to do?"

"Confront the source of what's troubling her."

Wonderful. The best thing in Nina's life would be if Ash moved out of her room—out of the house—and never came back again. And now she was supposed to help her cousin?

Ash sighed again.

"So where do I start?" she asked.

NINA

Nina woke, sitting bolt upright in her bed and clutching a tangled braid of sheets in a tight fist. Her nightie clung damply to her skin. Her body quaked with the aftershock of her nightmare. It was cold in the room. Icy cold. Her breath frosted in the air before her as she gulped for air.

Images cascaded through her mind.

The Zoo. The wolves. The attacking alpha male.

And Ashley.

Right there at the end, her cousin appearing in the middle of the pack, scattering them. Ashley and somebody else—only a vaguely remembered image of a veiled figure remained of her cousin's companion.

It *was* magic, Nina thought, shivering as much from fear as the cold. What else could you call Ashley appearing in her dream like that?

She shot a glance to her cousin's empty bed and her breathing literally died in her chest. She couldn't take a breath, could barely focus on what she saw, she was trembling so violently.

A tall, cloaked figure stood beside Ashley's bed. Hoary frost rimmed the floor where it stood. Pale flickers of snow drifted like dust motes in the air between them.

The figure spoke. It was a woman's voice, more hoarse than husky. Though Nina couldn't understood what it was that the woman said, the voice itself sent icy shivers prickling up her spine.

And she kept thinking: the magic's real. Her cousin was using magic against her—first to bring Nina her awful dreams, and now this. Sending some kind of a demon after her.

The figure spoke again, and this time the foreign words sorted themselves out in her mind so that she could understand what was being said.

You are mine.

Nina shook her head numbly.

You were promised to me.

"G-g-go aw-way. . . ." Nina managed.

Her teeth were rattling against each other and she could barely form the words.

Mine.

The figure took a step towards her and all of Nina's fears coalesced into one terrifying scream. It came up from her diaphragm, raw and tearing against her throat until it burst shrilly from her mouth. The figure hesitated. It seemed to shimmer, undulating like a reflection in a pool of still water into which a pebble had been tossed.

Then the door to Nina's bedroom opened with a bang and her mother was there. The figure vanished as though it had never been. There was no frost. No snow falling.

But the cold remained, rooted in Nina's bones.

As did the memory of the cloaked woman and her awful message.

You are mine.

You were promised to me.

Her mother crossed the room quickly and sat down on the edge of the bed, enfolding Nina in her arms.

"My God," she said. "You feel like ice."

Nina couldn't talk. All she could do was stare at where the cloaked figure had been standing and shiver.

"You're not going to school tomorrow," her mother said. "I should never have let you go today."

"I . . . I. . . ."

Her mother stroked Nina's hair, pushed the damp strands

away from her forehead. Slowly Nina's gaze moved from where her unwanted visitor had been to the doorway where her father stood wearing the same anxious expression as her mother.

"Everything okay in here?" he asked.

"She's got a chill," her mother said. "And she had a bad dream, didn't your sweetheart?"

Dream? Nina thought. If only it was all a dream.

"I'll go warm up a milk toddy," her father said.

"You'll be fine," her mother told her as he left the doorway. "You're just sick and you had a bad dream. It happens, Nina. It doesn't make it feel any less real, but it was just a dream. Do you want to talk about it at all?"

Nina swallowed thickly. "It . . . there was . . ."

Words just jumbled in her mind as she tried to explain.

"It was . . . Ashley," she finally managed.

Her mother sighed and continued to stroke Nina's hair.

"I know, dear," she said. "We're all worried about her."

"No, it's not that. It's just. . . ."

"You were dreaming about her?"

Nina nodded. "It was awful."

We just have to hope for the best," her mother said. "She's always had a stubborn streak about her, I just never expected her to pull something like this. God knows we've tried with her."

You don't know the half of what she's pulling, Nina thought.

"But," her mother went on, "at least one good thing's come out of all of this. It might not seem like a nice thing to say, but I have to admit that I'm happy to see you're worrying about her as well. I guess your subconscious knows how you really feel, even if you don't think you much care for your cousin."

"My subconscious?" Nina asked. She wasn't really sure what her mother was getting at. "What's that got to do with anything?"

"That's where dreams come from," her mother explained. "Sometimes dreams are just its way of telling us something that we don't really think we know."

"But I know—"

Her mother laid a finger against her lips. "Don't get yourself upset. What you need now is rest."

What was the use? Nina thought. How could she possibly

explain what was going on without her mother just thinking that she was making it up so that Ashley would look bad? Her parents certainly weren't going to believe in magic and spells anyway. She was having enough trouble believing in them herself. And even if she did manage to convince her parents that she was really seeing what she'd seen, they'd probably ship her off to see a shrink like they'd done with Ashley earlier this year.

"Here we go," her father said as he came back into the room.

He brought over a mug of steaming milk, laced with cinnamon, nutmeg and a dollop of brandy.

"Now you just drink that down."

Nina took it, grateful for the mug's warmth as she cupped her hands around it. The liquid settled in her stomach like tiny coals, their warmth spreading all through her body. The brandy made her feel sleepy.

"Don't you worry about getting up tomorrow morning," her mother said as she tucked Nina back in under the covers. "You just get as much rest as you can, all right?"

Nina nodded sleepily. She turned over on her side, pressing her face against the pillow after her parents had left the room. But though she was feeling drowsy, she doubted she'd be able to sleep. The milk toddy had banished the cold from her body, but the chill of what Ashley was doing to her, and the memory of that cloaked figure—

You are mine.

—continued to spread with like frost forming on a windowpane, brittle and thick.

What was she going to *do*?

When she finally slept, it was restlessly, constantly shifting from one position to the another, never really getting comfortable until the dawn began to leak its light into the eastern skies.

The next morning she was only vaguely aware of first her father slipping into her room to see how she was before he headed off to work, and then her mother, doing the same as she left for her studio. It wasn't until mid-morning that Nina came fully awake to the brittle jangle of the phone ringing at her bedside.

"I thought you were going to *tell* me the next time you skipped," Judy complained as soon as Nina muttered a sleepy hello into the receiver.

"I didn't know I was staying home until it was too late to call you," Nina replied.

"Are you sick for real?"

Nina wasn't quite sure how to answer. *Was* she sick for real? That depended on what was real. If she had just imagined that woman being in her room last night. . . .

"I don't know," she said finally.

"You had another dream, didn't you?"

"Yeah. And it was the worst one yet, because it was still going on when I woke up."

"You're not making much sense," Judy said.

So Nina explained the whole business: being a wolf at the Metro Zoo, the pack attacking her, but then scattering when Ashley and her mysterious companion had appeared, and finally waking up to the cold room, with the frost on the floor, snow in the air, and that horrible thing waiting for her there by Ashley's bed.

"Now do you believe me that it's Ashley?" she asked when she finished up.

"Not necessarily."

"Judy!"

"Hold your horses, Caraballo. I believe you had the dream. But maybe you were still dreaming when you thought you woke up—do you know what I mean? That's happened to me before, dreaming that I'm dreaming."

"I suppose . . ."

"But even if some kind of magic *is* going on, it doesn't sound like Ashley's causing it—not from what you've told me."

"But she was there at the zoo—checking out her handiwork."

"Sounds more like she saved your buns from those other wolves."

"I don't know about that," Nina said. "Sure, the pack took off when she appeared, but she just stood there staring at me. . . ."

Like she couldn't believe it was me, Nina suddenly realized as she played the scene back in her head. Like she was shocked to see me there, looking back at her through a wolf's eyes. But if Ashley wasn't responsible for what was happening to her, then who was?

She called up her memory of the cloaked figure standing by Ashley's bed. The image was easy to hold in her mind's eye. As was the woman's creepy hoarse voice.

You are mine.

Frost and snow. Right here in her bedroom.

You were promised to me.

She shivered. Was it getting colder in the room? Was that frost riming the windowpane?

"Nina, are you still there?"

Judy's voice, tinny sounding through the receiver, but comfortingly familiar, brought her back.

"Yeah, I'm here," Nina said.

"Are you all right?"

"Not really. It's like, if I'm not going crazy, then I've got some heavy-duty witch woman after me. I don't know which is worse."

"It's like in a fairy tale, isn't it?" Judy said.

"What do you mean?"

"What that woman said, about you being promised to her. You know how people are always promising their first kid to somebody or other in those stories."

"Thanks a lot. That makes me feel a whole better, thinking that my parents involved me in all of this."

"I didn't mean that they'd really done it. That's just in fairy tales."

"This *is* like being in a fairy tale."

"Do you want me to come over and keep you company?" Judy asked.

"Could you manage it?"

Judy's parents kept such a sharp eye on her that it required major preparations for just hanging out in the mall, never mind what it took for her to go out on a date or to skip school.. For the latter, a note had to be forged, which wasn't exactly the easiest thing in the world to do because Mr. Woo had very distinctive handwriting and a flourish at the end of his signature that was almost impossible to duplicate. Judy's younger brother Danny had made it his goal in life to perfect his father's signature. So far, his version was so good that the school secretary couldn't tell the difference, which, while it didn't satisfy him, was close enough for practical purposes.

"I'll get Danny to write a note for me," Judy said.

"Can you afford it?"

Danny didn't do anything for free.

"I don't have to," Judy said. "I caught him in the bathroom with a copy of *Playboy* last night. I told him then that a little blackmail can go a long way."

Nina couldn't help but laugh.

"He deserves it," Judy said. "Maybe I'll tell all the girls in his class anyway."

"You're wicked."

"But kindhearted where it counts. I'll be by after lunch, okay?"

"Thanks, Judy."

"Hey, what are friends for?"

Nina smiled as she cradled the receiver. The chill she'd experienced earlier was no longer in the air, and she felt a lot better knowing that Judy was coming over—enough so that she got up, put on a pair of jeans and a sweatshirt, and went downstairs to get herself something to eat. She got as far as the bottom riser of the stairs when the front doorbell rang.

Not thinking about what she was doing—"Never let strangers in when you're by yourself," her mother was constantly warning her and Ashley—she opened the door. Standing on the stoop was a complete stranger. He was maybe twenty, with short, dark hair and angular features, dressed in jeans, a white T-shirt and a long black leather raincoat. He looked kind of tough—enough so that Nina was already regretting just flinging open the door the way she had. But it was his eyes that really gave her the creeps. They were a pale blue—so pale they almost seemed colorless—and their intensity made her immediately uncomfortable.

"Y-yes . . . ?" she said.

"I'm looking for Ashley Enys," he said.

"I'm sorry, but she's not here," Nina told him and started to close the door.

The stranger put his hand against its oak panels, stopping her.

"It's important," he said.

His eyes glittered menacingly.

"J-just a sec and I . . . I'll get my dad. You can talk to him."

And she'd be out the back door and phoning the cops from next door so fast it'd make his head spin. But the stranger shot her feeble plan down before she could even give it a try.

"I don't think so," he said. "Your dad's at work; your mom's at her studio. It's just you and me, Nina."

Nina stared numbly at him. How did he know her name and where her parents were? More to the point, what did he want?

He pushed past her and walked into the house like he owned it. As soon as he was by her, she collected herself enough to try to bolt, but he caught her arm and pulled her back inside with him. Then he shut the door.

"No one's going to hurt you," he said. "I just want to ask you a few questions."

"Wh-why?" Nina asked, mustering what bravado she could "What are you? A cop, or are you just writing a book?"

The stranger laughed. "Maybe I'm a cop writing a book."

He walked her into the living room and pulled her down so that they were sitting together on the beanbag couch. He let go of her arm then, and she rubbed the spot where he'd been holding it, although it wasn't really sore.

"What do you want with Ashley?" she asked.

"Actually," he said, "now that I've met you, I think I was looking for the wrong one of you."

Great, Nina thought. Ashley attracts some fruitcake and now Nina was stuck with him. As if she didn't have enough to worry about right now.

As if she wasn't scared to death.

The stranger leaned back on the couch, folding his arms behind his head.

"So tell me about these dreams," he said.

Nina was so surprised that all she could do was stare at him.

ASH

Ash found that journeying through the spirit world with Lusewen was like taking a pleasant amble through her own memories of home. The ancient forest in which she first met her odd companion soon gave way to moorland, which in turn fell in a tumble of cliffs and rock-strewn inclines to the sea. The landscape could have been plucked straight from the northern coast of Cornwall—an area that she and her mother had hiked at least one weekend in every month of the year.

Lusewen guided her along the coastline, following a narrow track that twisted back and forth upon itself as it wound through the rocky common that lipped the cliffs. The air was thick with the salty tang of the sea. Lusewen's birds—the second was a goshawk, she said when Ash asked what kind it was—shared the skies with innumerable scolding gulls. The ground was springy underfoot, the earth thick and dark where it was caught between the ancient limestone formations.

"This place is like a dream," Ash said as they paused to look down at the view of a tiny cover that had opened suddenly before them. "Like it must have been back home, before the people came."

"We're the dream," Lusewen said. "At least in this place."

"What's that supposed to mean?"

Lusewen smiled. "Only that here, in this spirit world, we're less real than the world is itself. As its denizens are like ghosts when they intrude on our world, so we are the ghostly intruders here."

"The people I came with told me that the longer you're here in your physical form, the more dangerous it becomes," Ash said. "That you start to go a little crazy if you're here too long." She shot her companion a quick look. "Is that true?"

"You can always tell those who've journeyed often and long in these lands," Lusewen replied. "There's an otherworldly look in their eyes—a kind of mad light that makes them appear not quite all there anymore. They smile when there's nothing humorous. They seem to watch things move that aren't there. Such people are disconcerting to those who haven't traveled here; they make people uneasy, because madness—no matter how slightly it has brushed against someone—always seems dangerous to those who haven't known its touch."

Ash thought of Bones' eyes, and of her companion's—hidden behind her veil, but visible enough to reveal their brightness. Both Lusewen and Bones had that light in their eyes. They were both as much at home in this spirit world as Ash was in her own. Maybe more so. Then she remembered the man that had followed her home last night. She'd thought he had dangerous eyes, but maybe what she'd seen was just the light of the spirit world. Maybe he'd spent time here as well. Though that didn't explain why he'd followed her home from The Occult Shop.

"You said that mysteries were following Nina around," she said. "Why's that?"

"Because she carries a magic inside her."

Right. Ash was still having trouble thinking of her cousin as having any ability beyond applying her makeup just so and getting caught up in whatever was currently getting the hardest sell, be it the new Madonna album or some goofy TV show.

"No," she said. "I meant why do they do it?"

"Magic attracts them."

"Do I have that kind of magic inside me—the kind that would attract mysteries?"

Lusewen's eyes glittered behind her veil as she studied Ash for a long moment.

"Would that make you happy?" she asked finally.

Ash shrugged. "I'm not sure. It'd definitely make life a little more interesting. I mean, I look at what's going on around me in the real world, I think about what it's got for me, and I don't come up with a whole lot. At least with magic, I . . . I don't know. Maybe I could make a difference."

She thought of her mother. Magic could call her back, couldn't it? And then everything could go back the way it had been before she'd died. Normal. Not all screwed up the way it was now.

"You've got an attitude problem," Lusewen said.

Ash glared at her. Where did this fairy tale bimbo come off telling her that?

"Like you'd know all about it," she said.

"I know that things haven't been easy for you," Lusewen began.

Ash gave a quick bitter laugh. "Sure you do."

"But I *do* know," Lusewen said. "I've been where you've been. My mother died when I was young. My father abandoned me. And I've been where you are, too. Walking around with a chip on my shoulder, wanting so desperately to fit in, but not being able to because there were things in my head for which the kids around me just didn't have any frame of reference.

"The way I see it—the way I remember it when I was in your current situation—is that you've got two routes you can take. You can let your bitterness drag you down and make the rest of your life as empty or worse than it is right now, or you can make something of yourself."

Ash wanted to ask Lusewen about what had happened to her mother. She wanted to commiserate with her, to share the pain and maybe ease that tight, awful feeling that lived inside herself, but that unaccountable anger wouldn't let her breach the walls she'd erected between her inner self and the rest of the world. The walls were necessary. Because if you let someone in, you just got hurt. There was only one way to survive, and that was toughing it out on your own.

The two needs warred with each other. She could feel a part of herself reaching out to Lusewen—the soft part, the core hidden deep behind the tough veneer, the kid who'd been hurt one time too many. But when she spoke, it was the toughness that put a sneer on her lips.

"Oh yeah?" she said. "Like what?"

"What you're doing right now's a good step—helping your cousin."

"Big deal. Like I'm really doing the world a favor by helping little Miss Sunshine-and-light."

"You could take a lead or two from Nina," Lusewen said.

Which was what they said to her in school. Why can't you be more like your cousin? You've got so much potential, but you're just frittering it away.

The shrink that her aunt and uncle had sent her to hadn't been much better.

"I'm sick to death of hearing about Nina," she said.

"She's a good person."

"And I'm not?"

"I didn't say that."

"Yeah, well maybe it's easy to be like her. She got all the breaks."

"What do you mean?" Lusewen asked.

Her voice was gentle, soothing. And because of it, because— God knew why—Lusewen really seemed to care, Ash could feel tears welling up behind her eyes.

I won't cry, she vowed. I won't.

But her chest was so tight that it was hard to breathe and she could feel herself losing her grip on the tears.

"Nothing," she managed. "Let's ... let's just skip it. . . ."

"But—"

The grief was just too much.

"At least her parents love her! Okay? Is that what you wanted to hear? They didn't say 'We don't want you' or ... or go and die on her . . ."

And the dam burst. She turned away, tears streaming down her cheeks. Lusewen reached for her, but Ash jerked her arm away.

"Don't you touch me!" she cried.

She backed away until she was standing at the edge of the cliff, her body shaking as she wept. Lusewen kept her distance.

She stood with her arms hugging her chest, the raven on her shoulder, feathers ruffled in distress, the goshawk circling above her, filling the air with anxious, eerie cries.

"Your mother loved you," Lusewen said softly.

Ash only wept harder.

"She didn't want to leave you ... to go away the way she did."

At that the pain inside Ash grew worse.

"You do believe that, don't you?"

Ash could only nod. The tears wouldn't stop.

"And your father's just a jerk for not wanting you."

"E-easy for ... for you to say...."

"Come on, Ash, Lusewen said. She moved a few steps closer, her voice like a soothing balm. "The world's full of people like him. People who only think of themselves. People who won't take responsibility for things that they should. People who can't love ..."

Ash turned an anguished face to Lusewen, tears still streaming. When she spoke, her words came out in gulps between the tears.

"Then ... I guess I'm ... just ... just like him ... aren't I ... ?"

Lusewen closed the distance between them. She laid a hand on Ash's shoulder. Ash flinched, but she didn't draw away as Lusewen cupped her chin and lifted her head so that they could look each other in the eye.

"I don't believe that," Lusewen said.

"How ... would you know? You don't ... don't even know me...."

But the wind blew the veil back from Lusewen's eyes and something sparked between them. In that moment Ash felt as though the woman's gaze went right inside her. It was as though Lusewen could see every hidden crack and cranny that Ash had secreted away behind her protective walls. Could see all Ash had ever been or thought or done, weighed it and didn't find it wanting.

"You've made mistakes," Lusewen said, "and you've had bad luck, but in your heart—where it counts—you're a good person. That's enough for me."

Ash sniffled and wiped her nose against her sleeve. She didn't protest when Lusewen drew her into her arms and held her tight.

"It should be enough for you, too," Lusewen said.

It was a while before they went on. Lusewen took a charm from her bracelet. When she called it up into life, a small table appeared on the moor, lopsidely leaning against a limestone outcrop and laden with two mugs of tea and a plate of small cakes. Ash accepted the tea gratefully. She didn't think she was hungry, but once she tried a cake—they were sort of like honey and nut muffins, but had a heavy cake texture—she ended up eating four of them. When she started on a fifth, but found she couldn't finish it, Lusewen taught her the names of her birds and showed her the trick of calling them down onto her shoulder or arm to feed them.

The raven's name was Kyfy, the goshawk, Hunros—meaning "trust" and "dream" respectively, Lusewen explained.

"Why did you call them that?" Ash asked.

"To remind me to trust in my friends as well as in myself, and that when things get bleak, it's still possible to dream, to hope. Sometimes just thinking positively makes things get better, just as the inverse can be true."

"Attitude," Ash said with a faint smile.

"Something like that. Are you feeling better?"

Ash nodded.

"Enough to go on?"

Ash nodded again. She *was* feeling better, if oddly subdued.

As though in response to her mood, the landscape changed as they journeyed on. The moors became more bleak, the cliffs more forbidding. There were no birds now except for Kyfy and Hunros. The air grew progressively cooler until Ash had to button up her jacket. She glanced at her companion, but Lusewen didn't seem to feel the cold.

Hours later, after traveling through increasingly desolate heathland, they topped a small hill. Below them, hidden in a small valley, lay a forest of pine, heavy with snow. The wind coming up the hill to meet them had a winter's breath. Hunros landed on Lusewen's shoulder and complained in his high-pitched voice. Kyfy rode the cold wind in a descending circle until he, too, sought a perch. He chose Ash's jean-clad shoulder, much to her delight. She reached up a hand and tentatively stroked his gleaming black feathers.

"That's where she lives," Lusewen said.

Ash's momentary happiness fled. She wrapped her arms around herself, chilled as much from the cold as from the grim look of the forest. Catching her mood, Kyfy shifted nervously on her shoulder, talons gripping a little tighter than was comfortable.

"Who does?" Ash asked.

But she knew.

"Ya-wau-tse," Lusewen replied. "The spirit who has laid claim to your sister's soul."

Ash didn't even bother correcting her. Cousin or sister, she supposed it didn't really matter. She just looked down at the forest and shivered.

NINA

Lounging on the sofa, the stranger appeared completely relaxed. He acted as though the house was his and Nina was the intruder. It was a disconcerting sensation for her, but what made Nina feel even more rattled was that, for all the tough leanness of his features, he didn't seem very threatening at all, just lazing there.

Except for his eyes.

They were dangerous eyes. Spooky lights flickered in their depths, promising menace. They scared Nina so much that she couldn't move.

Please don't let him kill me, she thought.

"The dreams," the stranger said.

"Wh-who are you?"

"That's not really the question you want answered, is it?" he replied. "Or it's only part of it."

"What do you mean?"

"You want to know how I know all about you. What I'm doing here. What I want from you."

Nina nodded uneasily.

"My name's Alver," he said. "But you can call me Al—like in the song."

There was a mocking look in his eyes now.

I just want to call you gone, Nina thought. Out of my life.

"Doesn't help, does it?" Alver said.

She shook her head.

"I was following your cousin because she plays with magic," he said, "but you *are* magic."

"Me?"

Alver nodded.

"It's the magic that calls us—from the Otherworld. And it's the magic that made it easier for me to find you."

"Oh, come *on*," Nina said.

Her fear wasn't forgotten, but this was so preposterous that she couldn't help but protest.

"I'm about as magic as a piece of celery," she added.

Alver smiled. "Actually, certain Native People use the roots and seed of the celery plant as a stimulant and tonic, even as a nerve sedative. That's a sort of magic, wouldn't you say?"

His smile gave Nina the creeps.

"I suppose. But that doesn't make me magic."

"No. But what about your dreams?"

"What about them?"

"What do you think they are?"

Nina sighed. "A pain."

"And if I told you they were real?"

I'd think you were a fruitcake, Nina thought, but she realized she should be more diplomatic.

"I wouldn't believe you," she said.

"I see."

For a long moment then, he sat there without speaking. The mockery died in his eyes, replaced by a remote, almost melancholy look that made Nina think he was looking right through the walls of the house, off into unseen distances. As though he could see things there that nobody else could.

And they weren't very happy things.

"Let me tell you a story," he said. "Imagine there's a place, a faraway place that's not in this here-and-now, this world of yours, but is . . . someplace else. A valley, hidden from prying eyes even in that hidden otherworld. The people who live there are like the hamadryads of your Greek mythology—they live in the trees. They are literally a *part* of the trees. Mobile sensory units, if you will, for no matter how far they travel from their home tree, they still remain a part of it—some essential essence of them stays behind in the tree. And unlike the classical interpretation of these beings in your world, both sexes are represented."

Nina didn't like the sound of this. Imagine this place and its people, he'd said, but he didn't sound like he was imagining it. He sounded like he thought it was real. Like the way he kept referring to "your world" when he was talking about the only world there was. Or the bit about her being magic. Next thing he'd tell her was that these people kept the inside of their treehouses wrapped in tinfoil to hide them from UFOs and that Elvis was their literal king.

Crazy was fine. People could be as crazy as they wanted to be. But not like this. Not pushing their way into your home with their scary eyes to tell you weird stories. Because this kind of crazy was like the kind where the guy pulls out a gun and starts making his point by killing a few dozen people.

And since she was the only person here . . .

"Are you with me so far?" he asked.

Nina nodded quickly, not wanting to make him angry. "Uh, sure."

Play along with him, she told herself. Keep him happy.

She looked around the living room as he went on, trying to decide what she could use to hit him with—just saying she got the chance. She settled on a vase her mother had made in a ceramics class she'd taken a couple of years ago. It was solid enough to knock him down, but wouldn't kill him like hitting him with the hammer her dad had forgotten to take to work with him this morning might.

"Naturally," Alver was saying, "this forest would be the literal lifetime of these people. If their trees were to die, so would they. Their lives are dependent on the forest and its seasonal life cycle. In spring they blossom. Summer is a lively time. Autumn a fruitful harvest. In winter they sleep."

He paused and cocked an eye in her direction.

"Makes sense," Nina said quickly.

The vase was across the room, sitting on the table by the window. How many steps was that?

"The important thing to remember is that as these people

are dependent on the forest, so the forest is dependent on the seasonal cycle. It needs the winter to rest, to garner strength. It needs the summer to grow and drink the sun. The balance is significant. Without it, the natural order is upset and things ... change."

Nina's attention returned to him. He was no longer talking the way he had when he'd first come to the door, she realized. He still spoke English, but it had thickened with an indefinable accent. The cadences of his speech had changed as well, from a kind of streetpunky brashness to something more along the lines of the way her English teacher's voice sounded when he was reading aloud from a textbook.

"One year winter came to this valley," Alver continued, "as it does every year, following fast on the heels of autumn's harvest, but this time it didn't go away. This time it stayed. Year followed year, and still it remained. And do you know why?"

Because space aliens kidnapped a dwarf nun? Nina thought, but she wasn't stupid enough to say it aloud. Instead, she just shook her head.

"Because *she* had come."

Alver lapsed into silence again.

He really believes this stuff, Nina thought. Which left her in deep trouble. Her gaze flitted back to the vase, then searched the room looking for something that might be easier to reach if she got the chance. But it was the vase or her dad's hammer—one or the other. Anything else she could think of was just too far away.

"Who's 'she'?" Nina finally asked as the silence dragged on for too long.

Alver blinked and those pale eyes of his fixed her with their menacing gaze.

"Her name's Ya-wau-tse—that's a Kickaha word which means being-of-white-fire."

"I'm part Kickaha," Nina said, unable to stop herself from bringing it up. "My grandmother on my dad's side was a full-blooded Kickaha."

"I know."

"Oh."

Like it was a crime, Nina thought. Though maybe to him it

was. Who knew what was going on behind those spooky eyes of his? Maybe he had a thing against Native People no matter how thin the blood ran in them.

"Ya-wau-tse is an earth spirit," Alver said. "A winter spirit. Where she makes her home, the snow never leaves. Nothing can grow. The wheel of the seasons ceases to turn. And when it doesn't turn, then the wheels of our own lives can't turn either. We become locked in the stasis of winter. Our spirits wither and grow old without replenishment. We all become a little mad. Some of us die. In the end, we'll all die."

His voice was harsh, bitter. The eyes hard with pain and anger.

"Dying's part of another cycle—another wheel," he added. "We can accept that. But Ya-wau-tse brings it to us too soon. And too unnaturally."

He fell silent again, but this time the tension lay in the air thick enough to make Nina find it hard to breathe again. Her chest was so tight that her lungs just couldn't seem to work properly.

"I . . . I still don't see . . . ," she began.

"What it's got to do with you?"

Nina nodded.

"Even spirits aren't immortal," Alver said. "Most simply live out the span of their years, just as we do. But some have tasted worship and gained strength and even a longer life span from it. They come to need the nourishment of that worship. Otherwise they wither and fade away. They become addicted to the concept of immortality and their own power. When worship is denied them, they look for their nourishment in other ways."

Nina found him looking at her in a way that made her skin crawl.

Here it comes, she thought.

Her legs began to tremble.

"You . . . you're not thinking of . . . *feeding* me to her, are you?" she asked.

Alver shook his head. "Just the opposite."

Relief went through Nina, her tension easing like air escaping from a deflated balloon, until he reached a hand into the inner pocket of his raincoat and brought out a switchblade. A flick of the thumb and its stainless steel blade leapt from the handle with a sharp click that made Nina's pulse jump back into double time.

"I have to kill you so that she won't have a chance to feed on you," Alver said.

His voice was apologetic. The sadness in his eyes directed towards her, rather than the plight of his people.

All Nina could do was stare at the blade of his knife. Her entire being seemed concentrated on it. The way the light caught the steel. The shimmers of blue in the metal. The razor thinness of its blade.

"W-why . . . me . . . ?"

"There are prescriptions even for beings such as Ya-wau-tse," Alver explained. "She can't take a victim at random—only one that has been dedicated to her, and then only when that one has reached maturity. When she was worshipped, she could have taken any of her followers, for they were all dedicated to her, but at that time she didn't need to. Their worship sustained her. Now that she needs nourishment, she has only you."

"B-but. . . ."

"This isn't something my people and I are proud of. It's not something we want to do. But to survive, we have no choice. Ya-wau-tse withers more each day. If we can prevent her from feeding, she'll soon fade away and we'll be free. The wheel of the seasons will turn once more, and the wheels of our lives will turn with it. We would strike at her directly, but even in her weakness she is too powerful for us to win such a confrontation.

"I'm truly sorry."

As he started to reach for her, Nina backed as deeply into the beanbag sofa as she could to get away from him.

"You've got the wrong person!" she cried. "Nobody's dedicated me to anybody."

Except . . .

Not even Ashley? she asked herself, then realized just what stupid question that was. Like any of what this guy was saying was real. He was so smooth that she'd gotten caught right up in his little supermarket tabloid fantasy, but it wasn't real. All that was real was that he was nuts and she was about to die.

"Of course you were dedicated," he said in a reasonable voice that completely belied the knife in his fist, the hard grip of his hand as he grabbed Nina's shoulder and pulled her towards him. "Otherwise Ya-wau-tse wouldn't send your spirit totem seeking, now would she?"

At her blank look, he added, "You haven't been dreaming. Ya-wau-tse can only take you when you have found your totem— among her people that's the sign of maturity. That's why your spirit's been leaving your body and entering that of other creatures."

Nina numbly shook her head. "That . . . that's not true."

"For all our sakes, I wish it weren't. But it is. The proof lies before us. I can smell Ya-wau-tse's touch upon you. Someone dedicated you to her and now she seeks to claim that bounty."

Nina still shook her head. "W-who? Who did it?"

"I don't know who. It's usually one's parents, but it's not important, anyway. It's not relevant to the business at hand."

As he pulled her closer, she finally found the strength to struggle, but it didn't do any good. He was stronger than he had any right to be. He held her captive as easily as though she were just a toddler, ignoring the ineffectual blows that she rained upon his shoulders. The glittering blade of the knife rose up as he lifted his face, blinding Nina with the fear it woke in her.

"Please forgive us," he said.

"No!" Nina cried. She whipped her head back and forth, slammed her hands against him. "You're crazy! None of this is true!"

She heard a shriek then—a long, piercing sound that rang shrilly in her ears. She was sure that it was her own voice, until Alver lifted his head to look at the doorway where the sound had actually originated.

In his brief moment of distraction, Nina heaved desperately away from him and managed to pull herself free of his grip. She rolled to the floor and was on her feet in a moment, bounding to the far side of the living room before she turned to see what had interrupted Alver's attempt to murder her.

Judy stood there, hands lifted up to her face, eyes wide with shock. When Alver rose from the sofa, Judy turned and bolted, still screaming. Cursing, Alver followed her.

Now's my chance, Nina thought. I'll just slip out the back and call the cops.

Except there was Judy. If he caught her. . . .

Swallowing thickly, Nina grabbed the vase she'd settled on earlier ran quickly into the hall after them.

Judy had only managed to get as far as the front door where Alver had her pinned up against the wall. She was still screaming.

"Shut up, shut *up!*" he shouted.

Nina crept up behind him, the vase lifted above her head.

Please don't let me screw up, she prayed.

But just as she got near enough to hit him, some sixth sense seemed to warn Alver. He turned, pale eyes sharp with anger, an animal snarl on his lips. He started to lift a hand to protect himself, but he was too late. Nina swung the vase and it connected with the side of his head. There was one moment of his eyes widening with shock at the pain, then he dropped to the floor like a marionette with its strings cut. The knife dropped from his fist as he fell and went skittering down the hallway.

Nina stood over him, the vase held limply in her hands. Her fingers felt nerveless. They opened of their own volition and the vase dropped to shatter on the floor. There was a strange humming in her ears. It took her awhile to realize that it was the sound of her own blood, thrumming in the sudden silence that had settled in the hallway. She glanced at Judy, who was staring at Alver's fallen figure. Judy hugged herself, shivering with shock.

"Is . . . is he dead?" she asked.

"I don't know," Nina said.

"Shouldn't we find out?"

Nina glanced from Judy to the fallen man. There was blood on Alver's temple where she'd hit him. His chest didn't seem to be moving.

"I . . . I'm too scared to touch him," she said.

Judy nodded in agreement. "But . . . shouldn't we *do* something?"

Everything was a confused muddle in Nina's head. She was totally unprepared for the reality of what was happening. It was so different from how it seemed to work on TV or in a movie. The heroes in those shows always knew just what to do.

She was having trouble remembering how to breathe.

"I . . . I guess we should call somebody," she said finally.

Judy nodded again. "We should call the police—oh shit. I'm not even supposed to be here. My parents are going to kill me when they find out."

What a weird thing to bring up, Nina thought. Here they'd just survived an attack by a knife-wielding maniac, and Judy was worried about getting caught skipping school. Not that she was doing much better herself. Now that Alver was down and out, all of the weird things he'd been telling her came back to buzz around inside her head like flies batting up against a window.

Her spirit going totem-seeking.

Tree-people on wheels of time.

Someone dedicating her to an earth spirit.

"Nina?"

She blinked and looked at Judy.

"What if he comes around while we're calling the police?" Judy asked.

Nina nodded and finally stirred. "We'll have to tie him up."

"Even if he's . . . dead?"

"I don't think he's dead."

Nina didn't even want to *think* about having killed him. It didn't matter that he'd been ready to kill them. That part didn't seem quite real anymore.

"I'll get some rope," she said.

"I'm coming with you," Judy told her. "I can't stay here alone with him."

"Then you get the rope," Nina said. "I think my dad left some in the kitchen cupboard under the sink."

She had visions of them both going off and coming back to find him gone. *That* she couldn't handle at all. It'd be too much like one of those slasher movies where, no matter how many times the maniac is killed, he just keeps getting up and coming after the kids. . . .

She grabbed her dad's old baseball bat from the closet by the front door and stood over the fallen man, clutching the handle tightly, her knuckles whitening.

"Go on," she told Judy. "As soon as we get him tied up, I'm going to call my dad. He'll know what to do."

And then she could just collapse in his arms and stop pretending that she was brave.

"Okay," Judy said.

She edged by Alver's body and went into the kitchen.

Nina could hear scrabbling sounds as Judy looked for the rope. Her palms grew sweaty where they pressed against the tape-wrapped end of the bat. She kept thinking she saw Alver move—a finger twitch, an eyelid flutter. It took Judy three weeks to find the rope, another month to come back to the hall with it.

"Tie him up," Nina said.

Judy shook her head. "No way. *You* tie him up."

She exchanged the rope for the baseball bat and stood over Alver as Nina gingerly touched him, first with a toe to see if he'd move, then finally trussing him with the rope. By the time she was done, he looked like a cartoon heroine tied up on a set of railway tracks, the rope tied around and around him as often as its length would allow.

When she was finally done, she phoned her dad and then told Judy what Alver had been ranting about.

Judy shook her head slowly, looking from Nina to their captive as Nina spoke.

"I was just joking," she said when Nina was done. "About your parents promising to give you to the bad fairy."

"Don't *you* start," Nina replied.

"Yeah, but—"

"Besides my parents would never do anything like that, okay? The guy's just nuts."

"Then how did he know about your dreams? I sure didn't tell him."

"I . . ."

She gave Judy an anguished look.

"All that stuff he was saying . . . it can't be true . . . can it? People living in trees and evil spirits. It doesn't make any sense."

"You're the one who said that Ashley was a witch," Judy said.

"Yeah, but that was . . ."

What? Nina asked herself. Different?

She looked down at Alver. With his eyes closed, he just seemed to be sleeping. He still looked tough, but there was a kind of innocence about him as well.

"But how else could he *know?*" Judy asked. "About your dreams, about you and your family?"

Nina shivered. "I can't handle this."

And then her father came home. John Caraballo took one look at the trussed-up figure and then enfolded Nina in his arms.

"Jesus!" he said. "When you said there'd been a little trouble. . . . Are you okay, sweetheart?"

Nina nodded against his chest.

Stroking her hair, he looked over at Judy, the bat still gripped in her hands.

"How about you?" he asked.

"I'm okay now, Mr. Caraballo."

"Thank God for that," he said. "If the two of you can just hang in there for a moment longer, I'll call the police." He turned to Nina. "Did he say anything about Ashley? This has got to be connected to her disappearance. I've been a wreck at work all morning just worrying about her."

"Uh, Dad?"

"What is it, Nina?"

"Maybe you should hear what he had to say before you call the police."

Her father frowned. "What are you talking about?"

"Well, before this guy showed up, I've been having these weird dreams and the thing is, he knew all about them. I've only ever talked to Judy about them, and neither of us have told anyone else, but he knew just what had been happening to me in my dreams. And then he started talking about magic and Kickaha earth spirits and . . ."

Her voice trailed off at the confused look on her father's face. He gave Nina and Judy a considering look and sighed. Bending down, he checked Alver's bonds; then he sat down there in the hall with the two girls, Nina and Judy on one side of their captive, he on the other.

"Okay," he said. "I guess we can hold off calling the police for a couple of minutes. What did this guy tell you?"

*   *   *

Alver regained consciousness right near the end of Nina's story, though no one noticed until Nina had finished telling her dad the whole thing. It was Judy who first saw that Alver's eyes were open and watching them. She gasped and pushed herself as far back against the wall as she could to get away from him.

Nina knew just what Judy was feeling, but she didn't feel as scared anymore. Not with her dad there.

"They told me not to talk to you," Alver said to Nina. "They said, just do it, but I thought you deserved to know why."

Nina's father grabbed Alver by the lapels of his raincoat before Nina could respond and hauled him up from the floor until their faces were only inches apart.

"What've you done with Ashley?" he demanded. "What've you done with her, you miserable excuse for a human being."

"But I'm not human."

The calmly stated remark just made John Caraballo more angry.

"Where *is* she?" he cried.

He punctuated every word with a shake that was hard enough to rattle the teeth in Alver's head. Nina had never seen her father so angry before, and it frightened her almost as much as Alver had earlier. Her dad wasn't supposed to lose control like this. She reached across and laid a hand on her his arm.

"Dad," she said nervously. "Don't. . . ."

He turned to her, a stranger's eyes watching her for a long moment until the wild look finally cleared from his gaze. Slowly he lowered Alver to the floor, then held up his hands and looked at them in surprise. They were shaking.

"Jesus," he said. "Look at me."

"Dad, what if it's true?" Nina said.

Her father shook his head. "It's not possible. The kinds of things he told you about just don't exist."

"But my dreams . . ."

A troubled look touched her father's features.

"Totem dreams," he said softly.

From the way he spoke, Nina knew that the dreams had struck a chord in him.

"Do you know something about them?" she asked.

"My granddad—Nana Quickturtle's father—used to talk about them," he said. "Back in the sixties, when I was going back to my roots, like every other kid who had even a drop of Native blood in him, he told me about the two kinds of totems—the clan totem, the one that looks out for your family as a whole—and then the personal one, the one you have to go on a spirit journey to find. A shaman would put you into a special kind of a trance, and then your spirit was supposed to go walking, looking for that personal totem."

"Did you ever do that?"

Her father sighed. "I didn't know any shaman, but I used to . . . experiment with different things back then."

Which was another way of saying he'd tried drugs, Nina thought.

"Our clan totem was the catfish." He gave Nina a rueful look. "Not very exciting, is it?"

"Not very."

"So I tried to find my personal totem on my own. I was hoping for a wolf or a bear or an eagle—something impressive that I could talk up to people, you know? Or if not that—if it wasn't going to be something that was immediately special sounding to a non-Native—then at least something individual to the Kickaha, like the toad, which was supposed to be especially lucky, or the crow."

"What did you find?" Nina asked.

"Nothing. I just got high and risked the good health of my body for some stupid kicks. I was lucky. I didn't hurt myself. Not like some of my friends. . . ."

Nina could see unpleasant memories crowding in behind his eyes and knew he had to be thinking of some old friend who had become a junkie or ODed. She could never figure out why people took that kind of a chance with their health. It sure wasn't something she'd ever try herself.

John Caraballo shook his head. "Enough of this. It's time we called the police."

"I can prove it's real," Alver said as Nina's father started to rise. "I can take you to my world."

87

John looked at him. "It doesn't matter. Even if what you say is true—which I don't believe for a moment—what makes you think I'd sacrifice my daughter for your people?"

"Your jail won't hold me," Alver said.

"I'm betting it will."

"And even if it did," Alver added, "even if my people don't send someone else to complete the task I was set, your daughter's still in danger."

John's eyes narrowed dangerously. "Don't threaten me, pal. Don't threaten me and don't—don't ever—threaten my family."

"The threat doesn't originate with me—it comes from the earth spirit you dedicated your daughter to: Ya-wau-tse."

"I never dedicated my daughter to any ..."

But again his voice trailed off as more memories arose in a press behind his eyes.

"Jesus," he said softly.

"Dad?" Nina's eyes were wide with shock. "Is it true?"

"I ... it was never something I ever really thought about since those days...."

"*What* is it?" Nina cried.

"It was the summer you were born," her father explained. "Your mother and I were at a Renaissance fair—one to celebrate the middle of summer. We were more into the spiritual side of environmental concerns back then. The earth is our mother and that kind of thing. There was a big bonfire one night and we had an impromptu naming ceremony for you, dedicating your spirit to the good of the earth...."

Nina's features went white.

"Oh, jeez," she said. "Then it *is* true."

"Absolutely *not*," John replied. "Your mother and I were just kids back then, and we were into a lot of alternate lifestyles and belief systems, but we certainly weren't involved in any kind of a cult that would require the sacrifice of our daughter."

"Tell that to this Ya-whatever," Nina said.

"Ya-wau-tse," Alver said.

Both Nina and her father gave him a dirty look.

"Nina," John said. "All of this is just nonsense."

"Oh, yeah? Well, what if this Ya-wau-tse made the same mistake that Alver did and *she's* got Ashley?"

"I . . ." Her father shook his head. "It's not possible—not the mumbo-jumbo way he's telling it with earth spirits and other-worlds and that kind of thing. He might be involved in Ashley's disappearance, but it's the kind of involvement that's set right here, in our world. We'll let the police sort it out."

"You will see," Alver said.

"No," John told him, "*you're* going to see." He turned to Nina. "Can you watch him while I phone the police, sweetheart?"

Nina nodded.

"That's my girl."

As her father rose to his feet, Alver began to speak once more, but this time it was in a language that none of them could understand. He delivered the words with a nasal tonality, dragged the sounds of them together so that they bled into each other. Listening to him, little shivers of dread crawled up Nina's spine. As his voice took on a sing-song quality, sweat began to bead on his forehead. His eyes were tightly closed.

"D-dad . . . ?"

"It's going to be okay," her father said.

He hurried off into the kitchen to make the call.

Left behind, the two girls stared at their chanting captive.

"God, he really gives me the creeps," Judy said.

Nina nodded, but she didn't speak. She was scared again, because something was about to happen. She didn't know what, she just knew that there was more to Alver's story than a crazy man's ranting. The air in the hallway suddenly felt charged with electricity. Goosebumps marched up her arms and she couldn't help shivering.

"Nina . . . ?" Judy began, but Nina saw it too.

The air was getting cloudy. Mist was crawling out from under the floor where Alver lay and fogging the hallway.

"Dad!" she called.

That sense of something impending sharpened abruptly. By the time her father returned, his call still unmade, the hallway was thick with mist. They could still hear Alver's chanting, but it had grown soft as a whisper now—as though it came to them from some great distance.

"What the . . . ?" Nina's father began.

The chanting fell still.

Nina and Judy scrambled to their feet and stood behind John as he pressed forward, reaching for where their captive was hidden in the unaccountable fog.

There was nothing there for him to grab.

The fog cleared as precipitously as it had come. When it was gone, they saw that it had taken Alver with it. All that remained of their captive were the coils of rope with which they'd tied him, lying in an untidy heap on the floor.

Nine and Judy held onto each other, both shaking. Nina's father stepped forward and slowly bent down to pick up the rope. It hung limp in his hand as he turned to look at the girls.

"It's . . . it's just not possible," he said.

But the evidence lay there in his hand, plain for them all to see.

All Nina could think as she looked at that rope was, if Alver could do this, if he could magic himself away like this, then wasn't everything else true?

Otherworlds and totem seeking and earth spirits. . . .

Ya-wau-tse.

To whom her parents had dedicated her.

Withering and in need of new blood to rejuvenate her.

She was doomed, Nina thought.

The realization lay like a cold stone in the pit of her stomach. She looked at her father but could find no comfort in his own stunned reaction. The reality of Alver's magic seemed to have leached his strength from him.

Doomed.

ASH

"Do you know how to ski?" Lusewen asked.

Ash pulled her gaze away from the forest below to look at her companion.

"Not really," she said. "Why?"

"It would be the quickest way down the slope."

Ash nodded. The snow lay in a thick blanket over the valley and its surrounding slopes, puddled like porridge in a bowl. It was not going to be fun plowing through it. She drew her jacket more tightly closed. They weren't exactly dressed for the weather down there either, especially not Lusewen in her shimmery black dress and that long veil.

"I could learn," Ash said.

Lusewen laughed. "It's not the kind of thing you pick up in a few minutes. Never mind. I've got something else that'll do the trick."

She unfastened a charm in the shape of a small tepee from her bracelet and tossed it to the ground. As soon as the silver touched the moorland, the tepee grew up around them, enfolding them in its warmth. A fire burned low in the center, the banked coals surrounded by stones, the smoke escaping through the hole at the top where the support poles met. Thick furs lay on the floor. The smell of damp leather and smoke was strong in the air. The smokiness made Ash's eyes sting, but she was happy for the warmth.

"See if something fits," Lusewen said.

She indicated a heap of fur clothing that was piled up against one leather wall.

"How do those things work?" Ash asked.

"The charms?"

Ash nodded.

"They're magic," Lusewen said with a smile.

"I *know* that. It's just ... how can something so small and made of silver become full-sized and real? It doesn't make a whole lot of sense."

"Magic's like that. These charms work here, in the spirit world—in all aspects of the spirit world—but not in our own."

"Too bad."

"To each world its own wonders."

"I suppose."

Lusewen had outfitted herself in the clothing while they spoke, choosing a fur parka and leggings, a thick scarf and a pair of warm boots with the fur turned inside. Ash quickly followed suit. Except for a pair of boots that fit perfectly, the clothes she found were all a little too big.

"We look like a pair of Eskimos," she said as she wrapped her scarf around her neck.

"But we'll be warm," Lusewen replied.

Lying on the buckskin floor near another wall was a toboggan, which she picked up.

"All set?" she asked.

Ash nodded.

Lusewen made that odd movement with her fingers again and the tepee returned to its charm shape, taking with it its dark warmth. Ash blinked in the brighter light outside and took the toboggan from Lusewen while the older woman retrieved the charm and snapped it back onto her bracelet.

"How come this stuff—" Ash fingered the sleeve of her fur parka "—didn't disappear as well?"

Lusewen shrugged. "For the same reason that we weren't hungry after our meal earlier. I don't know what the charms are—where they came from or how they work; I just know how to use them." Taking the toboggan back, she set it on the snow at the top of the slope and added, "Do you want to sit in front or the back?"

"Definitely the front," Ash said.

Lusewen smiled. "I thought you'd say that."

The ride down to the forest was exhilarating. Kyfy and Hunros swooped above them, filling the air with sharp raucous cries that twinned the laughter that came bubbling up Ash's own throat. For the moment, troubles and trials were forgotten. She was breathless by the time they reached the bottom, and not even the gloomy umbra of the forest could dispel her sudden good humor. Right then it just felt good to be alive.

They got off the toboggan, dusting the sprayed snow from their parkas. Lusewen called up the tepee again and put the tobaggan inside, then returned the charm to her bracelet. While she was doing that, Ash studied the forest. Its brooding shadows worked on her nerves. Slowly her good feelings drained away.

"I feel like there's someone watching us," she said.

"There is. But don't worry," she added as Ash gave her a sharp worried look. "It's just the spirits of the trees. Don't break any of their branches and don't start any fires, and you'll do just fine."

Something in the way Lusewen spoke awoke an uneasiness in Ash.

"You sound like you're not coming with me," she said.

"I'm not."

"But—"

"This is your undertaking," Lusewen said gently.

She stroked Hunros's feathers where he sat on her shoulder, talons sunk deep into the pile of the parka's fur. Kyfy was still airborne, winging above them in high sweeping circles.

"Yeah," Ash said. "But all of this was your idea. I don't know anything about Ya-wau-tse. How do I find her? What do I do *when* I find her?"

"Finding her is easy. You'll see a path as you enter the forest—stick to it and it will bring you directly to her tower. But don't stray from the path."

"Or I'll end up in some other place?"

Lusewen nodded. "Or some other time."

"But what do I *do*? How do I defeat her?"

"We never spoke of combat," Lusewen said. "It was my understanding that you meant to rescue your sister."

"And how am I supposed to do that?"

"You could offer yourself up in her place."

Ash looked at her companion with a stunned expression. Lusewen merely returned her gaze with a mild look.

"You're serious, aren't you?" Ash said.

"It's an option."

"Great option. It just means that Nina gets it all again and I get nothing. I lose everything."

"Or maybe you'll gain . . . everything."

"You're not making a whole lot of sense," Ash said. "If giving yourself up to Ya-wau-tse's a good thing, then why don't I just let Nina benefit from it?"

"Because she's not doing it willingly."

"And that makes a difference?"

"The choices we make always make a difference."

"You know what I meant."

Lusewen nodded. "And you know what I mean."

Ash turned to look at the forest again. Snow hung heavily on the branches of the pines. Except for the sound of their own breathing, the stillness was absolute. Beyond the first few trees, the darkness became impenetrable. Ash looked back at her companion. Kyfy had finally perched and was preening his feathers on Lusewen's other shoulder.

Lusewen undid the clasp that held her bracelet and offered the charms to Ash.

"This belongs to you now," she said.

"To me?"

Ash took the bracelet gingerly. The charms were still warm from Lusewen's touch.

"Can I use one of these to defeat Ya-wau-tse?" she asked.

Lusewen shook her head. "The charms are for creating, not breaking. You can find or fashion more to add to the bracelet, remembering only that they must be true silver and they must not be a symbol of any form of undoing. If you add one such as that to the bracelet, it will become what it is in our own world: only jewelry once more. Here, as well as at home."

"I'll be careful."

"To give the charm life," Lusewen continued, "you must keep an image of what you are calling up firm in your mind. And this—" she did that odd movement with her fingers again, but slowly now, so that Ash could easily see how it was done "—is how you return what you called up to its aspect as a charm."

Ash nodded her understanding, but she was having trouble concentrating now. As she held the bracelet a memory rose up in her mind that refused to be ignored.

In her mind's eye, she saw Cassie sitting on the marble bench in the Silenus Gardens, laying out the cards on the bench between them as she had earlier in the day before all this weirdness had begun. The ninth card, the one that was supposed to represent her own hopes, had been an image of her trying to top a summit where there were no more handholds. Reaching down had been a helping hand. And—she remembered now—on the wrist connected to that hand had been a charm bracelet.

This charm bracelet, she realized. It had to have been this bracelet.

Which meant that it had been Lusewen, reaching down to her.

"Who are you?" Ash asked.

, Lusewen smiled. "Still looking for a compartment into which you can neatly fit me?"

"No, really."

"I'm who you might be."

Ash hefted the bracelet in her palm. "You mean I could become a magic worker like you?"

"A thousand—a thousand thousand—possible futures lie ahead of each choice we make," Lusewen replied. "Each of them becomes a world of its own where the person who made the decision to create it carries on her life."

"Are you saying I could?"

"Who knows? In one of them you could. Anything is possible, especially here—in this place."

"But does it last when you go home?" Ash asked. "Or does it just become fairy gold—leaves and dirt?"

"That depends on who takes what back," Lusewen said.

Reaching into her pocket, she took out that curious pomegranate with its iconic silverwork. She held it up to her eye for a moment, then handed it to Ash.

"This is for you as well," she said.

"What is it?"

Lusewen shrugged. "Whatever you want it to be."

"Don't talk like that. Please. You're not making any sense."

"Remember what I told you about this place when you first found me?"

Ash nodded. "That it's the spirit world that's crazy, not the people in it."

"Just so. But it can make you crazy. That's the trap. It tries to remake you to be like it is, rather than what you are. You have to be strong."

"But—"

"Good luck, Ash."

"Wait a minute," Ash said. "Don't go."

But she was too late. Lusewen took a step to one side and disappeared as though she'd stepped between the folds of an invisible curtain.

"You can't leave me here!" Ash cried. "I'm just a kid."

A wind arose on the heels of her words, dusting the snow around her.

So were we all once, she heard whispered in its passage.

The wind died down.

Silence returned.

And she was alone, standing there amongst the snow drifts on the edge of the forest.

She set me up, Ash thought. This whole thing was a set-up. Lusewen was working with Ya-wau-tse.

She looked down at her clenched left fist. Slowly she opened her fingers and studied the charm bracelet that lay there on her palm. Then she looked at the weird piece of . . . fruit jewelry, was all she could think to call it.

Nothing made sense anymore.

She didn't know who or what to trust anymore.

Lusewen had seemed like the perfect friend. A little weird at first, but once she'd gotten to know her better, Ash had felt a real affinity towards the woman. She'd felt she could trust her—spooky eyes, magic, birds, and all. Lusewen had seemed to really care about her—not just how she did in school, or how she got along with other kids, or whether she helped out around the house and was in on time, but about *her*. What she felt. Her hopes and aspirations. Her fears. . . .

Ash had opened up to her as she'd never opened up to anyone before—not even Cassie.

And now Lusewen had just abandoned her.

Like her mother had.

Like her father had.

This is your undertaking.

Right. Like she could do it on her own.

It was my understanding that you meant to rescue your sister.

Like Nina'd ever do the same for her.

You could offer yourself up in her place.

Sure. Sacrifice herself for Nina who always got what she wanted.

No way.

Maybe you'll gain everything.

Ash looked down at the bracelet again.

Everything?

Magic wasn't everything, she realized at that moment. Magic was only a tool; you used it to help achieve your goals, but it was the doing, the learning, that was the most important, not the end result. That's what all the serious books she'd read on the subject told her. It was the journey, not the destination, though you needed the one to embark on the other.

And, in the end, you had to do it yourself. People could give you directions, map out some good routes, but you had to actually do it yourself.

That was what Lusewen was saying, wasn't it? That was why she'd taken off the way she had.

Ash wanted to believe that, because she wanted to trust the mysterious woman. She needed to trust in someone.

She needed real friends.

Sighing, Ash fastened to the bracelet to her wrist. She dropped the pomegranate into her pocket and turned to face the forest again.

So naturally, she thought, she'd gone and picked another person like Cassie, who was off mooching around as much as she was there to hang out with. But friends didn't always have to be right there beside you for you to know that you had their love and support, did they? And when you had to do something on your own . . .

Did she even want to do this?

No way.

But Lusewen had shown her this much: She was so wrapped up in what she felt was wrong with her life, so centered on its negative aspects, so ready to just let everything slide and give up, that she never even tried to make it better. Anybody with an ounce of authority over her was automatically the enemy. And everybody was . . .

When she hung out with Cassie, all she did was talk about her own problems. She really didn't know much about her friend. Like why an obviously well-educated woman would choose to live on the streets and be a fortune-teller.

The kids she hung out with—well that was all surface, wasn't it? Copping attitudes and being cool. Being tough.

And Nina.

Looking back—if she was going to be honest about it—Ash knew that her cousin had really tried to make her feel at home when Ash had first come to live with the Caraballos. Ash just hadn't given her a break, and so Nina, naturally enough, had simply met Ash's hostility with her own.

Could they ever be friends? Did she even *want* to be friends with someone like Nina with her just-so hair and magazine ad outfits, her sappy music and her perfect grades?

But that wasn't really the point, was it?

You did something like this *without* trying to figure out what you could get from it.

You just did it.

The forest swallowed her as soon as she stepped inside. The path Lusewen had indicated was easy to follow, winding through the trees like an unspooled ribbon. The snow wasn't deep under the canopy of pine boughs, but the cold seemed to sneak in under her furs and cut right through to her bones. With each step she took, she could feel the gazes of the tree spirits settling more and more heavily upon her. Don't break a branch or light a fire, and you'll be fine, Lusewen had said, but Ash sensed that the trees harboured spitefulness towards her just because she was intruding in their space.

Stray from the path?

No way. Not in this place. She'd learned that lesson already when she'd gotten separated from Cassie and Bones. She didn't need to try it again. In this world, it was just too easy to get lost. Who knew what the next world she ended up in might be like? But if she made it through this confrontation with Ya-wau-tse, she was determined to learn all the ins and outs of traveling through the Otherworld.

She wondered if her eyes were already getting that weird gleam in them like Lusewen's and Bones's had.

She thought about how nice it would be to just be lying in her bed, reading a book, The Cure playing on her Walkman.

She kept on walking.

And tried not to worry.

About Ya-wau-tse.

About what she was going to do when she was finally face-to-face with the earth spirit.

Her calves had developed a fierce ache in them by the time the path ended in what she supposed was a glade. The forest had thinned somewhat as she approached it. It had become a grave-yard of trees. Huge pines lay in a tumbled tangle, their needles browned and dead, their boughs broken from their falls—the larger trees pulling down smaller ones in their wake. The path twisted through the wreckage, then ended in what felt like an opening, but it was hard to make out exactly what lay ahead. Winds blew blinding veils of snow at the edge of the forest, making it impossible to see more than an arm's length in front of her.

Ash paused there, shielding her eyes from the wind-driven snow. She was reluctant to step into the storm.

If Ya-wau-tse was a winter earth spirit, Ash thought, then this had to be where she lived. And if this was where Ya-wau-tse lived, then Ash knew she'd reached the end of her journey. What she didn't know was if she could go on.

We never spoke of combat, Lusewen had said.

Well, that was good, because Ash didn't feel strong enough to take on a mouse. But the other option Lusewen had given her . . . to offer herself up in Nina's place . . .

That would take a courage that Ash didn't think she had.

The dread of this moment had been growing steadily stronger in her, with each step she took along the path. And here, now, at the end of the journey, she was frozen with fear as much as the cold. She couldn't move.

Come on, she told herself. Don't be such a chickenshit. Where's the street tough who's got an answer for everything and everybody?

Ash knew where she was.

That kid didn't really exist. She was just a construct to hide the hurt. To keep from being hurt more.

Fine, she thought. So make the change. Just do it.

Shivering, Ash drew in a frosty breath, and stepped into the veil of snow, only to pause again. This time from surprise.

Gone was the forest and any trace of it. Gone was the snowstorm, if not the snow. It lay thin on the hard ground. The wind remained as well, gusting small clouds of the granular snow against her skin, then sweeping across a plain that stretched for as far as the eye could see in all directions. And there, a half-mile or so from where she stood, was a structure that was oddly familiar. It took Ash a moment or two to realize that it was the tower from the Tarot reading Cassie had done for her in Fitzhenry Park.

It had been the fifth card.

The one representing her near future.

Well, that future was here now.

Just get it over with, she told herself.

She was about to move forward when a footstep in the snow behind her made her turn quickly, pulse hammering. Her fears weren't relieved when she found herself confronting the man who'd followed her home from The Occult Shop last night.

He looked different here. His hair was still cropped short, but he was dressed in furs and leggings much like what she wore, instead of that street punk outfit she'd first seen him in. His hands were thrust into his pockets.

His eyes hadn't changed at all. Their gaze fixed on her with a menacing intensity.

"You," Ash said. "What are you doing here?"

Had everybody walked between the worlds before except for her?

"I live here," he replied.

"Yeah. Right."

"It's true. The real question is, what are *you* doing here?"

Ash nodded at the tower behind her.

"I'm trying to rescue my cousin," she said.

The stranger sighed. He brought his hands from his pockets. In the right one was a knife.

"Then I'm here to stop you," he said.

NINA

Gwen Caraballo sat quietly at the dining room table after her husband and daughter had told her their story. Nina regarded her with a kind of awe. It was obvious from her mother's thoughtful, if somewhat worried, expression exactly what she was thinking.

"You believe us, don't you?" Nina said.

That surprised her. Nina had been there when it was all happening and she still wasn't sure if *she* believed it. If someone had come to her with this story . . .

"Of course I believe you," Gwen said. "I know what you've told me sounds impossible, but you're the two people I love the most in the world and if I can't believe in you, then who can I trust?"

"Jeez," Judy said. "I wish my parents were more open-minded."

Judy had absolutely refused to go home. What had happened here was scary, she explained, but it was even scarier to think of being at home by herself. She knew that the spooks hadn't been chasing after her, but she didn't want to take the chance that, now that they were aware of her existence, they wouldn't come after her as well. No one could help her at home. Her parents would never understand.

"Maybe you should give them more of a chance," John said.

"I try all the time," Judy replied. "Just with ordinary things like going out on a date, but they're too Old World."

Nina's father nodded. "I hear you."

He was the one who had called Judy's mother to ask if Judy could stay over for the night.

"So what do we *do* now?" Nina asked.

"Call the Ghostbusters?" her mother replied with a faint smile.

"Not funny."

"I know." Her mother sighed, then turned to her husband. "Maybe we should call the police again to see if they've learned anything new."

John shook his head. "I've already phoned them three times this afternoon. The last time they said they'd call me as soon as they had word, so could I please just let them get on with their work."

For once Nina didn't find herself thinking something along the lines of, don't worry about Ashley being missing, worry about some ice queen coming to get *me*, because, oddly enough, she was feeling worried about Ashley herself. Here it was, just what she'd always wanted—Ashley gone and her parents belonged to her alone again—but now all she wanted was to have her cousin back. She felt guilty for ever wishing Ash ill because she couldn't stop the little nagging voice in the back of her head that kept reminding her that she was partly to blame.

For always wishing that Ashley would just get out of her life.

For having some spook running after her and Ashley getting caught up in all the trouble just because she was her cousin.

Because that was what must have happened.

This Ya-wau-tse must have grabbed Ashley. . . .

"What are the police going to know about magic lands and earth spirits?" Nina asked.

Her father sighed. "There's that."

"What we need is a wizard," Judy said.

"Or a shaman," John said.

Nina felt a surge of excitement. "Do you *know* any?" she asked.

Her father shook his head.

"We could ask around, though, couldn't we?" Gwen said.

"There's a woman at the health food store who's always talking about healing crystals and past lives."

"And there's that store where Ashley buys all her creepy books," Nina added.

"I'd feel like a fool," John said.

"They won't think you're foolish," Gwen said. "Not if they really believe."

"What about the guys from the Renaissance fair?" Nina asked. "Like whoever it was that organized my naming ceremony?"

"God, I just can't believe this is all because of that," her mother said. "That was all so innocent. Peace, love, and flowers...."

"There's a lesson here," John said. "It just brings home the simple truth: You've always got to take responsibility for everything you do, no matter how trivial or frivolous it seems at the time."

Nina rolled her eyes. Please, she thought. Not the responsibility shtick again. If she'd heard it once, she'd heard it a thousand times.

"But what about those fair guys?" she asked, hoping to circumvent the lecture before it started.

"The Wiz—Peter Timmons," her mother said. "He's the one who organized stuff like the Maypole dancing and that naming ceremony."

John nodded. "Only the last I heard, he was in Morocco."

"Again?"

"More like still. Wendy mentioned that she got a card from him a few months back. Seems he never left."

"Well, what about Paul Drago? Didn't you work on a job with him last winter?"

Winter. At the mention of the word, a chill cat-pawed up Nina's spine. Was it cooler in the room, or was she only imagining it? She looked nervously around herself, but then realized that it couldn't be Ya-wau-tse. She only came when Nina was sleeping ... didn't she?"

"This isn't getting us anywhere," she said.

Her mother laid a hand on her arm. "I know, honey. But this is all new to us. We don't know *what* to do. The only way we can work something out is by talking to someone who maybe does know."

"But these people you're talking about, they're just. . . ."

She let her voice trail off as she realized what she'd been about to say.

Her father smiled. "Old hippies? Like us?"

"Well . . . yeah."

"Just because we were all idealistic back then, doesn't mean that everything we believed in was nonsense."

"I know. But that was all sort of spacey stuff—back-to-the-earth philosophies and things like that. This is real."

"Environmental concerns are pretty real," her father said. "Helping out those less fortune than ourselves, the way the Diggers did back then, that was real."

"So was promising your kid to an earth-spirit!" Nina blurted out, then quickly put her hand in front of her mouth.

Her parents both looked hurt.

"I'm sorry," Nina said. "I didn't mean that to sound the way it did."

"I don't have an excuse for what we did," her father said. "Saying that we didn't know any better doesn't mean much, does it? Not now."

"I know you didn't do it on purpose," Nina said. "That you didn't know this stuff was all going to happen. It's just that . . ."

She shivered, feeling a chill that seemed to settle in the marrow of her bones.

"I'm really scared," she said.

"So are we, honey," Gwen said.

"But I feel so cold right now . . . it's like she's coming for me again. . . ."

Her parents exchanged worried glances. Judy started to tremble as well, though she was only scared, not cold.

"Nina . . . ?" John said.

As he leaned towards Nina, his face got all blurry in her vision.

"So cold . . . ," she said.

She could feel his hand on her arm. It was hot. Not like the room. The room was like the inside of a freezer. She could see her own breath every time she exhaled. A sprinkle of snow drifted through the air above the table. No one else seemed to see it.

"She's like ice," she heard her father say, but his voice came as though from very far away.

"Oh, my God," her mother said, her voice growing more and more distant too. "What should we do?"

There was another hand on her arm—another hot touch.

"Nina, honey," her mother was saying. "Can you hear me?"

She tried to nod, but her head felt so heavy. It started to drop to the table, falling ... slow, slow. The cold touched every part of her. She had a ringing in her ears. The room smelled like a winter's day. And then she was drifting away.

Into the cold.

Into the cold dark.

She heard her mother shriek her name, but it was like a pinprick of sound in a vast ocean of shadowy silence.

And then she was gone.

Into that cold darkness.

She blinked her eyes open to a bizarre new perspective. She was in another body again. An animal's body. But this time it was different. This time it felt ... right.

She was in a weird forest of tall green growth that took her a few moments to realize was only grass. Her new body was fat and squat, the skin dry and wrinkled, but there were powerful muscles in her hind legs and she felt attuned to her new shape in a way that made it feel more familiar than her own body.

The cold was gone.

Bunching up her legs, she gave an experimental hop. Her borrowed body answered with a grace that made her grin with pleasure.

She was a toad.

And she felt just fine.

Looking for a totem, she thought. Now that she had found it, she wondered why she'd ever been scared in the first place. The toad's body, the odd scurrying way its mind worked, the way it instinctively understood its relation to itself and everything that existed, brought her a sense of peace that left her breathless.

This wasn't scary; this was beauty—the way her dad had used the word once when he was talking about the Native concept of everything being in its proper place, all the connections made and understood. A kind of inner harmony that, when you had it, reflected that beauty out into one's surroundings.

And hadn't her dad said something about a toad totem being lucky?

Well, she felt lucky. All those old terrors were gone—the alien bodies, the clumsy way she'd tried to make them move, the utter dread she'd felt trapped in their flesh. . . . All that was gone.

Until she heard the footsteps.

Until the monstrously huge shape loomed over her, an old wrinkled face as wide as a house bending towards her, leviathan fingers reaching down to pluck her from her haven in the grass.

Ya-wau-tse.

"Welcome, daughter," the spirit said.

Again the words were in some alien tongue, but again Nina could understand them.

"Now that I have helped you learn who you are, it is time for you to help me."

Nina's pulse thundered, the tiny toad heart rattling inside her chest like a frenzied drum.

"No need for fear," Ya-wau-tse said. "There will be no pain. It will be like falling asleep—falling into the forever where your ancestors' spirits wait to greet you. Be joyful. The Wheel turns. You will step upon it again."

I don't want to die, Nina screamed silently.

"There are worse things than dying," the spirit told her. "There is living without hope. There is never having known love. There is never learning who you truly are. Your life has been short, little daughter, but you have known all these things and more."

The fingers that gripped her were like icicles. The cold numbed Nina so that her amphibian body grew drowsy. She caught a glimpse of a building, recognized it as her own house.

She was in the body of a toad in her own backyard, she thought sleepily. That seemed funny for some reason—odd funny, not ha-ha funny.

The cold was stealing away her fear, stealing away her ability to think at all. Her drowsiness was a balm that called her into sleep's dark embrace.

Like falling asleep, Ya-wau-tse had said.

Falling into forever. . . .

A part of her tried to muster up the energy to fight off the sleepiness. It tried to warn her of the danger, but she was too tired to listen to it. By the time Ya-wau-tse stepped from her backyard into the Otherworld, Nina had let the darkness take her away.

John rose from where he was sitting and caught his daughter's head just before it hit the table. He cradled her against his chest. Her muscles were slack, arms hanging loosely like the floppy limbs of a rag doll.

"She's freezing," he said. "It's like she's . . ."

He didn't say the word, but it hung there in the room between them all the same.

Dead.

He tried to feel for a pulse, fumbling at her wrist, not really knowing what he was doing.

"What are we going to do, what are we going to do?" Gwen was crying.

"We don't panic," he said, hugging the cold, limp body of his daughter closer to him. "We . . . Jesus, I don't know. . . ."

Gwen was at his side now, brushing the hair back from Nina's icy brow.

"We have to take her to the hospital," she said.

She felt as though something inside her was dying as she looked down at her daughter's ashen features.

And then the doorbell rang.

Nina's parents looked at each other, neither quite grasping what the sound meant.

Sitting numbly at the table with them, Judy was still shivering as well, fear riding up her spine like the clawing grip of a nightmare that wouldn't let her go. Why hadn't she just gone home? She didn't want to be here. She didn't want to see Nina looking like this. She didn't want to know anything about magic or any of this awful stuff.

The doorbell rang again.

"I ... I'll get it," she said.

Anything to get out of this room where the smell of death seemed to be gathering thicker with each passing moment.

She opened the front door and stared at the two strange people that were waiting on the step. A black woman and an Indian. The woman looked like she'd just stepped out of one of the sidewalk vintage clothing and jewelry booths in Crowsea market and was wearing half its wares. The man looked like a Foxville punk, except he was too old. His eyes were so like Alver's had been that Judy took an involuntary step backwards.

"Muh—Mr. Caraballo!" she cried.

John appeared in the hallway, Nina in his arms. He didn't know this pair any better than Judy did.

"Who are you?" he said.

"We're friends of your daughter," the woman replied. "We ..."

The man pushed by her and Judy and hurried to where John stood holding his daughter.

"I don't have time for—" John began.

The man reached over and laid his palm against Nina's forehead. He glanced over his shoulder at his companion.

"We're too late," he said. "She's already taken her."

"I *told* you we should've come right away," the woman said.

"What the hell's going on here?" John demanded. "Who are you people?"

"Friends of your daughter," the woman repeated.

"Which daughter?" Gwen asked.

She'd come into the hallway as well to stand beside her husband. When Judy sidled down the hallway towards her, she put her arm around the girl's shoulders and hugged her close.

"Ash," the woman said. "My name's Cassie—Cassandra Washington. And this is Bones. We knew of the danger Nina was in, but we didn't think it was as immediate as this."

"I don't have time for this crap," John said. "Get out of my way. I have to take my daughter to the hospital."

"What's wrong with her, they won't be able to cure in a hospital," Bones said.

"Yeah? Well, I'm taking her all the—"

"Look at me," Bones said. He spoke in a voice that would brook no argument, his eyes flashing dangerously. "What do you see?"

A crazy Indian, John thought, but the words died stillborn because he knew exactly what Bones was. He couldn't have put into words how he knew; he just did.

"Blood calls to blood," Bones said. "You know I mean you no harm. How could I? We are kin."

Before he even knew what he was doing, John was bending his head in respect to the shaman.

"My . . . my daughter," he said.

"I will try to ease her passing," Bones replied, "but it is with the living we must concern ourselves now."

"We need something that belonged to Ash," Cassie said.

Gwen just looked at her numbly. What the shaman had said was only barely sinking in.

Ease her passing. . . .

"Nina . . . ?" she said.

"Do you want to lose both your daughters?" Bones asked her.

"Wh-what's going on here?" John asked.

All the belligerence had gone from his voice. The man who spoke now seemed only lost.

"It's a long story," Cassie said. "One we really don't have time to get into right now."

Bones took Nina gently from John's arms. Skinny though he was, the weight of her limp body seemed of no consequence to him.

"Bring me something of Ash's," he said as he carried Nina into the living room. "Something she cared about."

"I . . . ," John began, but then he nodded and hurried up to the girls' room.

"Nina," Gwen said in a small voice as she followed Bones into the living room. "Will she . . . is she really . . . ?"

Cassie remembered the reading she'd done for Ash. The blank outcome card lay heavily in her mind. She hoped to God that it didn't mean that Ash was going to end up the same as her cousin.

"Miss . . . uh . . . Cassie . . . ?"

Cassie looked at Ash's aunt and her heart went out to the woman. Gwen was in shock right now. Her eyes had a glaze to them and she moved with stiff, jerking motions as she knelt down by the sofa where Bones had laid Nina down.

Cassie helped Judy sit down in a chair, then joined Gwen by the sofa. She laid her hand comfortingly on the woman's shoulder.

"Bones," she said. "He's the best at what he does. He's going to do all he can for her."

She hated herself for the false hope she was handing the woman, but what could she do? There was still Ash to think of.

Ash, lost somewhere in the Otherworld.

They should never have taken her across with them, never let her get mixed up with any of this. But the juju had been working on this family all along. Just check out the poor girl lying there on the couch.

Damn, why couldn't they have come sooner?

She'd argued with Bones about it all afternoon.

"We can't just not do anything," she'd said.

"We are doing something. We're looking for Ash. That's our primary responsibility."

"But her cousin . . . ?"

Bones had sighed. "What can we do? Do you think her family is going to welcome to us when we come knocking on their door? It's only going to sound like some cock-and-bull story to them. First thing they'll do isn't listen to us, Cassie. What they'll do is call the cops. We're not exactly citizens, so where do you think we'll end up?"

Busted, Cassie thought. Because they were homeless. Street people. Never mind that they'd chosen this life for themselves, where others had it thrust upon them. Citizens had jobs, lived in homes, paid taxes, and looked on the police as their employees. Got a problem? Call the cops. Living on the street, you didn't have the luxury of calling in the men in blue when things got a little hairy. You dealt with it yourself. As best you could.

And when it was juju . . .

Bones was right. They couldn't go to the Caraballos. But

when she thought of what would happen when that spirit chasing Ash's cousin finally caught up with her . . .

"Don't worry," Bones said, knowing what she was thinking. "It's not like the spirit's going to move on her today or anything."

Cassie had nodded and let Bones get back to the task of tracking down where Ash was in the spirit world, but the afternoon dragged by without success. As evening fell, Bones finally gave up.

"I need something that belonged to her—a personal possession," he said. "It'll give me the extra focus I need to cut through the veils. They're layered thick today—lots of action going down in the spirit world."

"I don't have anything," Cassie said.

Bones sighed. "Then it seems we have to pay a visit to the Caraballos after all. Do you have their address?"

Cassie shook her head. "It's somewhere in Lower Crowsea. We can look up the street and number in a phone booth on the way."

"Hold on," Bones had said. "Ash may be lost in the spirit world, but I should be able to track down where she lives in this world."

Where there weren't so many conflicting folds of time overlapping each other, Cassie thought. Or manitou playing tricks with one's perceptions.

Bones closed his eyes, fingers playing with the dream crystal that hung from the belt loop of his jeans by a beaded leather thong. Cassie was prepared for a longish wait, but Bones's eyes flickered open only a brief moment after he'd closed them. He rose quickly to his feet.

"Come on," he said, tugging Cassie up from the floor and then down the hall of the tenement in his wake. "Do you have money for a cab on you?"

"Sure," Cassie replied, worry flaring in her. "What's wrong?"

"The spirit is coming for Ash's cousin."

"Tonight?"

Bones shook his head grimly. "Right now."

They'd lucked out on a cab as soon as they hit Gracie, but it took them too long to find the Caraballos' house because Bones couldn't give the driver a street address, just directions.

Turn right here, straight for so many blocks, take a left. . . .

By the time they'd arrived, it was too late. The spirit had come and taken Ash's cousin away into the spirit world, leaving only an empty shell of a body behind. No longer animated by its soul, it would soon die.

Cassie looked down at the stricken girl and her heart went out to her. Poor kid never even knew what was happening to her, she thought.

Ash's uncle returned then, holding a battered old teddy bear in his hand.

"She always loved . . . she loves this old guy," he said.

Bones glanced at Cassie, who took his place by Nina's side, gently stroking the stricken girl's icy brow. If there was only something she could do. But herbs could only help so much when you were dealing with this kind of heavy-duty juju. Still, if she could ease the girl's passing . . .

"Boil me some water," she said to the mother. "Can you do that?"

Gwen nodded dully and left the room. While she was gone, Cassie reached into her shoulder bag and took out a small cloth sack that was filled with packets of dried herbs, each individually wrapped in brown paper. Behind her Bones had taken the teddy bear from Ash's uncle and was sitting cross-legged on the floor now, the toy bear on his lap, his eyes closed.

He lit his pipe. Smoke wreathed about him, growing thicker than it had any normal right to. Judy and Ash's uncle stared wide-eyed.

Bones began to chant.

He talked to the smoke, cocked his head as though listening to its reply. By the time Gwen returned with a bowl and the kettle, steam still wafting from its spout, the smoke was dying down.

"I can't find her," Bones said.

"Well, try again," Cassie said.

Bones gave her a quick look at the sharp tone of her voice, then nodded and lit his pipe again. Cassie chose a packet of herbs. Filling the bowl with boiling water, she steeped the herbs in the liquid, then held the bowl up under Nina's nostrils so that the steam could enter the girl's system, riding in on the back of her shallow breathing. The steam brought a little color to Nina's cheeks and her breathing deepened slightly, but otherwise there was no response.

Gwen crouched on the floor beside Cassie, her trembling arms hugging her knees. Judy sat in the chair to which Cassie had led her and didn't seem able to speak or move. John was on his knees on the floor in front of Bones, staring hopefully into the smoke that was wreathing around the shaman.

Cassie could tell by the look on Bones's face that he wasn't having any more luck finding Ash than she was in reviving Nina.

She closed her eyes tiredly.

Oh, man, she thought. Had any of them ever had a worse night?

ASH

"Hey, look," Ash said. "Can't we talk about this?"

The stranger shook his head. "I'm done talking with you and your family."

Say what? Ash thought.

She eyed his knife without looking directly at it and took a small step back. The stranger immediately closed the distance between them.

Keep him talking, Ash told herself. Until you can think of something.

Good plan. Great plan. Think of *what*?

"What's that supposed to mean?" she asked. "Who *are* you anyway?"

But then she remembered the trees—those old pines in the snowy forest that had been watching her. Watching her with the same kind of malevolent gaze as lived in his eyes.

He had to be one of the tree spirits.

"You live in the trees," she said. "You're a—" she searched for the word Bones had used, found it "—a manitou."

The stranger shook his head. "We are not the little mysteries— merely the spirits of the trees. Manitou have powers such as shaman have, only they are born to them, born of smoke and drum magic. My people are little different from you, except that we live longer ... and in trees."

"Whatever," Ash said.

She tried not to look at his knife, just wanted to keep him talking.

"I didn't light a fire or break any branches," she added, remembering what Lusewen had told her about the forest, "so why do you want to hurt me?"

"My name is Alver," he said, speaking slowly, as though to a child. Only his eyes betrayed his impatience. "There is a spirit living in that tower; her name is Ya-wau-tse. She once lived free as the manitou always have, but then she tasted worship and stepped from the turning of her Wheel. The worship sustained her, raised this tower for her, changed her perceptions of her place in the natural order of the world. But her followers died off, and now she withers and seeks the soul strength of your cousin to sustain her."

"I know all that," Ash said. "Why do you think I want to stop her?"

"Where Ya-wau-tse dwells," Alver went on as though she hadn't spoken, "it is always winter. Branches are laden with ice and snow; the frost pierces deeply into the ground. Her winter is killing us."

"I get it," Ash said. "If she dies, her hold on you's gone—right?"

Alver nodded.

"But if she gets Nina—my cousin—then she's just going to be strong again."

"Exactly."

"So what's your problem with me? We've both got the same enemy."

"You can't defeat her," Alver said. "If it was so simple a thing to do, my people would have accomplished it years ago."

"But—"

"And even if you *were* able to rescue your cousin, Ya-wau-tse will merely pluck her from your world again."

Ash remembered what Lusewen had said just before she'd disappeared.

We never spoke of combat.

No. To save Nina she wasn't supposed to try to fight Ya-wau-tse. Lusewen had this real brilliant idea.

You could offer yourself up in her place.

Somehow Ash didn't think that would go over too well with bright-eyes here.

She fiddled with her charm bracelet, wishing that it didn't have the limitations that Lusewen had told her it did. Forget wishing there was an Uzi or sword or any other weapon charm. Just a shield would be nice right about now.

"So you've talked to Nina?" she asked. "And to my aunt and uncle?"

"To Nina, your uncle, and another girl."

"And . . ." Ash swallowed dryly. "What happened?"

Alver touched the side of his head, fingers just fluttering against the skin, not really touching. But he still winced. Looking closely, Ash could see blood matted in his short hair. She hadn't noticed that before. She'd been too busy trying not to look at his knife or his crazy eyes.

"Uncle John did that?"

Alver shook his head. "No. Your cousin did."

Way to go, Nina, Ash thought. I never knew you had it in you.

"I won't be caught so easily again," Alver went on.

Ash took another step back.

"I'm sorry," he said as he followed her.

Yeah, right.

"Look," she tried again, but suddenly he was in motion.

The knife came at her, Alver's arm moving faster than Ash would have thought was possible. She sucked in her stomach and tried to throw herself to one side, but the knife got snagged in the folds of her parka. As Alver started to pull the blade free, she shoved at him with both hands. He slipped on the snow and went down, taking her with him. She turned as he fell. The knife, still caught in her parka, pulled out of his hand.

He hit the ground hard. Ash managed to block her fall with her arms. The shock of the impact rocked her all the way up to her shoulders, but she pushed herself away—out of Alver's scrabbling grip. His fingers caught the pocket of her parka, the pocket ripping as he tried to pull her towards him. Ash kicked out at him, but he'd suddenly stopped his attack.

Ash scooted away from him on her hands and knees, pausing when she'd put a few feet between them. But he didn't seem to be interested in attacking her anymore. All the fight had gone out of him. Instead he was staring at what had fallen from her pocket when he'd torn it. The hard gleam in his eyes softened with awe.

The pomegranate with its iconic silverwork lay there on the snow between them. Closer to her than to him. Slowly his gaze rose to meet hers.

"Where did you get that?" he asked.

"Screw you."

"You don't know what it is, do you?"

"Sure I do."

"Liar."

"So tell me," Ash said.

"The silverwork speaks of Grandmother Toad—she whose Wheel is the moon—while the fruit itself is the heart of the spring. Its shape and internal structure are a symbol of the reconciliation of the multiple and the diverse within apparent unity. Worked together as they are here, they promise Wheels brought back into their proper balance no matter how far they have strayed from their initial turnings."

Ash thought of Lusewen's birds. The raven, whose name meant trust; the goshawk, whose name meant dream. Lusewen, it seemed, was big on symbology. She touched her bracelet. These charms were symbols as well.

Only how was she supposed to put it all together?

"So?" she asked.

Alver blinked. "This is a powerful fetish. It can heal; it . . . the blood it carries within it will heal our forest."

Thanks a lot for filling me in on all of this, Lusewen, Ash thought.

"You mean it'll break what's-her-name's hold over you?"

Alver nodded.

"So take it," Ash said. "It's yours. Now will you just leave me alone so that I can—"

She broke off at the look that came over Alver. Utter terror

118

swept across his features. A moment later she was aware of the footsteps crunching in the snow behind her. Alver shot a glance at the pomegranate, then scrabbled to his feet and fled. Disappeared. Just like Lusewen had.

Dreading the idea of doing it, but knowing that she didn't have the same option as Alver had to just conveniently vanish, Ash turned around. Approaching her was a living version of the image from the foundation card in Cassie's reading.

Ya-wau-tse had the most wrinkled brown skin Ash had ever seen. She wore the same beaded doeskin dress with its fur mantle that she'd been wearing in the picture on the card. Her eyes were even more compelling in real life—deep, bottomless brown pools, quarries of dark water that had no bottom. The small cowrie shells and beads woven into her braids made faint clicking noises as she moved closer to stand over Ash. Little flurries of snow danced around her feet, although there was no wind that Ash could feel. The spirit-woman carried her staff with its headpiece of feathers in one hand. In the other she held a toad.

She spoke, but the words were just so much gibberish. Sparks flickered in the back of her eyes and Ash felt a buzzing in her head, but when the spirit-woman spoke again, she could understand her.

"Well," Ya-wau-tse said. "What have we here?"

There seemed to be a faint rumbling in the air. Ash put it down to the thundering rhythm of her own pulse until she realized that it came from outside herself. It was like far-off thunder.

Or drumming.

Ash got slowly to her feet. "I . . ."

"But I see you are kin," the spirit-woman said as Ash's mouth grew all gummy and wouldn't work properly.

"K-kin?" Ash managed.

"Distant, but kin," Ya-wau-tse assured her. "Be easy, child. I won't harm you."

Oh, yeah? Ash thought. Then why did she feel like she was about to die?

Even with her parka, leggings and boots, and the long scarf wrapped around her neck, she was suddenly freezing. Something sparked off the spirit-woman—a kind of invisible cold fire that licked at Ash's bones, chilling them to the marrow. Now she knew what Alver's frozen trees must feel like. And she was supposed to offer herself up to this woman?

Think of Nina, she told herself. Nina wasn't like her. There'd be no big loss to the world if something happened to her—who'd miss her anyway?—but Nina . . . Nina had everything ahead of her still. She was smart and she fit in.

Not like me, Ash thought. I've got nothing.

All she had was her anger. And her loss.

"I . . . ," she said. "I've come to . . . to offer a trade."

Ya-wau-tse's eyebrows rose questioningly.

"Me. Take me instead . . . instead of my cousin. To . . . you know . . ."

The drumming seemed to have grown louder, but now Ash was sure that it was just the sound of her own pulse thrumming against her inner ear.

Ya-wau-tse held up the toad. "I already have what I need," she said.

Ash looked at the creature in the spirit-woman's hand, not understanding. The thing seemed comatose, a tiny, limp, wrinkled creature held in a hand that was, if anything, even more wrinkled. But then it stirred, its eyes blinking open, and Ash saw those eyes.

Her heart stopped for one long deadly moment.

Oh, jeez.

That was Nina trapped in there. Nina trapped in that toad's body like she'd been caught inside the wolf before.

Totem-seeking . . .

"B-but . . ."

Ya-wau-tse gave a short sharp laugh that sounded like a coyote's *yip-yip-yip*.

"Go home, child," she said.

Then, before Ash could reply, the spirit-woman brushed by her, heading for the tower, snow eddying in her wake. The drumming continued—sounding like distant thunder again. Fading.

Ash stared numbly after the spirit-woman. This wasn't the

way things were supposed to work out. Lusewen hadn't said anything about Ya-wau-tse refusing....

"You can't not take me!" she cried.

Ya-wau-tse never turned, never acknowledged that she heard.

Ash picked up the pomegranate and thrust it into the pocket that Alver hadn't torn. She stared at his knife, but left it lying there. What did she know about knives? The idea of just holding it scared her. She'd never be able to use it.

She got to her feet.

"Listen to me!" she cried after Ya-wau-tse's retreating figure.

Still no response. It was as though Ash no longer existed for the spirit-woman.

"You can't treat me like this," she muttered. "I'll *make you listen.*"

Oh, really? And how was she going to manage that?

But she started after Ya-wau-tse, pausing only when she thought she heard her name being called. She looked around the snowy plain and listened carefully, but then realized it must just have been her imagination.

Or an odd echo of the drumming.

She hurried after the spirit-woman, determined to come up with some course of action to help her cousin before Ya-wau-tse did something worse to Nina than turn her into a toad.

Ya-wau-tse reached the tower before Ash did. When Ash got there, she couldn't find a door, couldn't even find the spirit-woman's footsteps in the snow. There was only one set of prints marking the snow—her own. The tower reared above her, round and tapering upward, dwarfing her into insignificance with its bulky height. The structure's round walls were made of hewn stone. They were pocked and weathered, worn with wind and age, grey and veined with quartz. The stones were set snugly against each other with only hairline cracks to show where the one ended and the other began. Not only was there not a door, there was no opening to be found at all—not even a window.

Not at all like the tower on Cassie's card with its tiers of windows, high up on the wall.

Ash kicked a booted foot against the stone.

"Let me in," she cried.

Still no reply. The building might as well have been deserted.

Ash looked back the way she had come. She could find no trace of the snowstorm through which she had stepped to reach this place. There were only the plains, spreading as far as the horizon, desolate and cold. The air crackled with the promise of a coming storm. Thunder rumbled—but no, she thought as she listened to it. Snowstorms didn't have thunder and lightning, did they?

Nina would know if that was possible. Nina the amazing toad girl . . .

Ash turned back to the tower and pounded a fist against the stone.

"You've got to take me!" she cried.

Why should I? a disembodied voice asked her.

Ash stepped back from the wall and looked around her. Though she couldn't see the spirit-woman, she recognized Ya-wau-tse's voice. Her ears buzzed with a faint dissonance.

The rumbling sound, thunder or drumming or whatever it was, grew steadily close. It was still soft, but there was a sense of nearness about it now. As though the drummers were just a thought away.

You care about nothing, Ya-wau-tse went on. *If you live or die, it is all the same to you. What would I want with a spirit such as yours? You don't need me to take you from your Wheel. You have already stepped from it yourself.*

"That . . . that's not true."

That you care about nothing, or that you've stepped from your Wheel?

Ash sensed a mocking humor in the spirit-woman's voice that infuriated her.

"Neither's true!" she cried.

So, Ya-wau-tse's disembodied voice replied. *Then what can you offer me, child—child who cares so strongly?*

The spirit-woman spoke with heavy irony.

"I do so care," Ash said. "It's just . . ."

She thought of her mother.

Gone.

Her father.

Another kind of gone, but just as permanent.

She'd loved them both.

Her friends.

She could count them on one finger.

Cassie.

Her aunt and uncle.

Taking care of her out of obligation.

Nina.

They hadn't got along from the word go.

"People just don't care about me," she said.

The spirit you offer me is as withered as my own grows, Ya-wau-tse said. *Why should I want it?*

"Because ... because I'm offering it to you freely."

That does not make it much of a bargain. A hard, unloving spirit in exchange for this one of your cousin's, filled to repletion with its love for life. And for those in her life. Even for you, child. She even has room to love you.

"I ... I love her, too!" Ash cried, realizing only as she spoke the words that they were true.

Then remember her with that love.

"Just take me instead."

What you have is not enough, Ya-wau-tse replied .

Ash fell to her knees and laid her brow against the stones.

"Please," she said. "I have to be enough. I'm all I've got."

There was no reply.

"Please ..."

Her voice trailed off as she realized that the spirit-woman's presence was gone again. She pressed her forehead against the stones, hard enough to hurt, and stayed like that for a long while, the cold settling into her, snow blowing up against her face, caking around her eyes and mouth.

The drumming was almost gone now.

Slowly she stood up, failure bowing her shoulders.

Wasn't that the worst of it? She'd failed because she just wasn't good enough.

Well, it wasn't news—was it?

That's what her father thought for sure. And the dim bulbs who passed for student counselors at school, pretending to care about the kids. And that psychiatrist that her aunt and uncle had sent her to.

They were all the same. They'd all come to the same verdict. She wasn't good enough.

Uncle John and Aunt Gwen, they must feel the same, too, or else why send her to see the shrink?

She stuck her hands in her pockets. One hand could find no purchase because the pocket she put it in had been torn. The other closed its fingers around the pomegranate. She took it out and looked at it, tracing the silverwork with her gaze. What was it that Alver had said about this combination of fruit and silver? Something about it being a fetish. About when the two were combined. . . .

They promise Wheels brought back into their proper balance no matter how far they have strayed from their initial turnings . . .

"Well, balance this," she said to the fetish.

Cocking back her arm, she threw it as hard as she could at the wall of the tower. It struck with the sound of an enormous bell being rung. All around her the fading sound of the drumming suddenly intensified. The fruit was just a smear of juice and pulp on the wall now, its peel and the silverwork lying in the snow at its base.

The juice looked like blood, dripping down the stones.

Ash took a step closer. She put her knuckles to her mouth and couldn't tear her gaze away from the dripping.

It *was* blood.

The tower was bleeding.

The drumming intensified until her head ached with it.

Her gaze followed the slow passage of the blood to the ground. Where it touched the snow, steam arose. Greenery appeared in the steam, shoots of grass and then a flower—the small yellow blossom of a buttercup. Hissing and crackling as it grew from the thawing ground, the greenery spread like spilled water. Sweetgrass and clover, dandelions and bunches of violets, purpose flowers sparkling. Shrubs grew in the wake of the ground cover. Saplings, crowned with tender new shoots and buds that unfolded into leaves with a speed only duplicated by stop-motion photography. The air was thick with the sudden heady scent of spring.

Healing, Ash thought. That's what Alver had told her the pomegranate fetish would do. Heal the land.

But the tower ... Cracks seamed the stone wall facing her. The shifting of the stone sounded like ice breaking on a river in spring. Rumbling came from deep underground. The tower swayed, rock powder dusting the air.

Ash backed slowly away, fear clawing at her nerves.

With a boom like a sharp crack of thunder, the stones she'd struck with the fetish fell in on themselves. For a moment, Ash's vision went black. When she could focus again, Ya-wau-tse stood there among the broken stones, wreathed in stone dust.

The spirit-woman's features were more ravaged than they'd been before, reminding Ash now of a picture of a mummified corpse she'd seen in an issue of *National Geographic*. It was as though all the liquid in her flesh was evaporating. Her eyes flared with dangerous lights. She still held the toad in one hand. She pointed her staff at Ash.

"What have you *done*?" Ya-wau-tse cried.

Frost gripped Ash's chest. It froze the air in her lungs. Stopped her heart. Make her bone marrow swell so that her bones felt as though they were cracking with fissures.

"I ... I ..."

She couldn't speak. She could barely make a sound. Everything was a shimmery haze of frost and ice.

"You malicious little child," the spirit-woman spat. "I'll—"

"Do nothing," a new voice said.

Ya-wau-tse slowly raised her head to look beyond Ash. As soon as her gaze left her, Ash found that she could move again. She sucked a ragged breath into her tortured lungs. Hugged herself with trembling arms. Slowly turned to see what had interrupted the spirit-woman from finishing her off.

And found who had been responsible for the drumming she'd been hearing.

There were people standing in a half circle around the spirit-woman and herself—or at least Ash thought they were people at first. People dressed in leather shirts and leggings, men and women both. Beadwork decorated their bandoleers, the medicine pouches hanging at their belts and the belts themselves.

And they all wore masks.

There was a fox with a feathered headdress. A bear with grizzled braids. A raven with a beaded headband. A turtle with a brightly coloured scarf worn on its head like one of the old Italian ladies in Foxville. A tree frog, skin speckled green and yellow, wearing a black, large brimmed hat. A hawk with an antlered headdress. A mouse in a little beaded cap. A catfish, a hare, a moose.

And a wolf with a crown of rose briars.

"You have no right to interfere," Ya-wau-tse told them.

"She has given us the right," the bear-woman replied.

Ash stifled a gasp of surprise.

Those weren't cleverly-made masks. Those were their real heads. . . .

"She has called us," the fox-man said.

"Who . . . who are you?" Ash asked in a small, wondering voice.

"Dreamers," the mouse-woman said.

"We fill the spirit-realm with our dreams," the frog-man added.

"We show dreamers their Wheels," the raven-man said.

Their voices woke the same buzzing sensation in Ash's head as Ya-wau-tse's voice had, but she felt no danger with these animal people. She regarded them with delighted wonder, noted the drums hanging from their belts, the fingers that strayed to them—first one player, then another—and kept the simple rhythm of their sound thrumming in the air.

"You're totems, aren't you?" she said.

The wolf-woman inclined her head gravely. "We guide," she said.

"We watch," the hawk-man said.

"We dream," the moose-woman added.

"You interfere," Ya-wau-tse told them.

"No," the catfish-man said. "We are merely here to see you off on your long-delayed journey."

"And to make certain that you do not take those whose time has not yet come with you," the turtle-man added.

"I am going on no journey," Ya-wau-tse assured them.

"Look at yourself," the hare-woman said.

The mummifying process had continued while they spoke. Ya-wau-tse's flesh was only dry withered skin clinging to her bones now. Her eyes were sunken hollows. Her lips thin to the point of disappearance. She held up Nina in one skeletal hand.

"She will renew me," she said.

She held the toad to her brow, pressed the tiny creature against her wasted skin and began to chant. The fingers of the animal people all strayed to their drums. Music arose from their instruments—a stately, yet joyful, sound. Its rhythm played counter to Ya-wau-tse's chant, diffusing its power, washing it away.

The air was warm now, the plains bright with green growth. The tower was just so much broken stone, heaped like an enormous cairn behind the withering spirit-woman.

"You murder me," Ya-wau-tse said.

The wolf-woman shook her head. "No. It is merely your Wheel, turning once more. Quickly, quickly—to capture all the years you have stolen from your alloted span."

"Your time will come again," the hawk-man said.

"I won't be the same."

The hare-woman laughed quietly. "Why should you? You have already stepped this Wheel; it is time you learned another."

"I . . ."

But Ya-wau-tse could no longer speak. The dried flesh holding her jawbone in place gave way and the bone tumbled to the ground. Ash stared at in horror, shivering as the woman became only so much dust and bone that fell to the green earth in the jawbone's wake. The catfish-man caught Nina before she struck the ground and solemnly handed her to Ash. The turtle-man retrieved Ya-wau-tse's staff from where it had fallen and broke it across his knee. He thrust the two halves into the ground—broken ends pointing down. When he stepped back from them, the broken halves of the staff grew a webwork of branches, which burst into bud.

"Farewell, sister," the frog-man said.

Ash held the toad that was her cousin gingerly in her palm.

"So . . . that was all I had to do?" she asked. "I just had to break the pomegranate?"

The mouse-woman shook her head. "The fetish was a cata-lyst," she said, "but it required a sacrifice before it could become effective."

"First you had to die," the raven-man explained at Ash's blank look.

"But I . . . never . . ."

"Are you still who you once were?" the wolf-woman asked gently.

Ash slowly shook her head.

"So," the turtle-man said then. "Now do you understand?"

"The . . . the old me . . . died? And now . . . now I'm a new me . . .?"

"Just so."

Ash frowned. "But . . . that seems too easy. . . ."

"Has it been so easy?" the wolf-woman asked.

Ash shook her head again. No. The changes she'd gone through inside herself had been anything but easy.

"And the task will grow harder still," the hare-woman said. "For you must now maintain what you have so recently earned."

"You mean, be good to other people and do what I'm told and that kind of thing?"

The catfish-man shook his head. "No. Just be true to your-self. Anything else of worth will develop from that."

"Welcome the days to come, rather than wait for them to come to you," the hawk-man added. "Or you will become as Ya-wau-tse aptly pointed out—the same as she was. But you will be withered before your time, rather than long after."

Ash touched a finger softly along the back of the toad, marveling at how soft the skin felt. Nina's eyes looked back at her from the creature's broad face. They were full of trust.

"Can I . . . can I talk to my mum?" Ash asked.

"She is not here," the bear-woman said. "She has already stepped onto a new Wheel."

Ash tried to hide her disappointment, but her throat grew thick and she had to look away to conceal the brightness that tears woke in her eyes.

"Be glad," the moose-woman said softly.

Ash looked up. Through the film of her tears, the animal people seemed like so many dream shapes. No longer real.

"Glad?" she said.

The turtle-man nodded. "Her song has no ending, child. We are all part of the same song—your people, our people. That song goes on forever. Our individual strains will always be a part of it, no matter what Wheel we step."

"So she's . . . she's okay?"

"Of course she is," the wolf-woman said. "The pain exists only for those left behind. Put it from you. Remember her with joy—great joy—but let her hold on you go."

Ash nodded slowly. No one spoke for a long time then. There was just the drumming. Ash let her pulse twin its rhythm until that desperate feeling inside her started to ease a little.

"I guess I've got to go back now," she said. "To bring Nina back. All this must be pretty scary for her."

"Not now," the raven-man said. "Not now that Ya-wau-tse has journeyed on. Your sister revels in her totem shape, for in it, she sees the world, and her place in it, as it truly is."

Ash never thought to correct the raven-man about her relationship to her cousin. She just accepted that they were siblings—as she should have years ago.

"Do I have a totem, too?" she asked.

"Look for it," the frog-man said.

"In dreams," the wolf-woman added.

She took something from her pocket and attached it to Ash's charm bracelet. It was a tiny silver wolf's head charm.

"We will be here to help you find it," she said.

The drumming grew softer now. Ash stirred, realizing her surroundings for the first time in a while. The plains were gone. She and the animal people stood together in a glade. All around them, green and growing, were the trees of Alver's forest. She could sense the tree spirits in the trees, watching them—no longer malevolent, just curious.

When she looked back at the animal people, they didn't seem as sharply focused any more. It was as though they were starting to fade.

"Why didn't you stop her yourselves?" she asked.

"Ya-wau-tse?" the fox-man said.

Ash nodded.

"It wasn't ours to do," the hare-woman replied. "When humans meddle with manitou, they must stand responsible for their actions."

"We can only watch," the moose-woman said.

"And wait," the raven-man added.

Their voices were growing more and more distant. Ash could see right through them now.

"Is Lusewen one of you?" she asked quickly.

There was so much she needed to know.

"No," the catfish-man said.

"But she is a dear friend," the wolf-woman said.

They were almost gone now—just vague ghostly outlines remained.

"Will I see you again?" Ash cried.

The animal people's outlines disappeared. Faint drumming replied, faded, was gone. But there was promise in its rhythm.

Ash looked down at the toad in her hand.

"Well, kid," she said. "It's time we went home."

She felt light-headed, capable of anything.

"And how're we going to do that?" she asked Nina rhetorically. "Just you watch."

She placed the toad on the ground and took off the fur parka, letting it fall to the grass, then sat down to remove her leggings and boots. It was sweltering here now compared to how it had been when Ya-wau-tse was in control. Calling up the tepee with its charm, she stowed away the winter gear, then returned the tepee charm to her bracelet. Sorting through the other charms on the bracelet, she finally found the one that she knew would be there. A tiny silver image of a Lower Crowsea house, complete with its tiny-postage stamp of a backyard. She got it free from the bracelet, then picked up Nina and stood up.

"Here we go," she said.

But before she could toss the charm down and wake its spell, a figure stepped from the trees on the far side of the glade.

Alver.

There was no knife in his hand now.

But his eyes still held that spirit-world wildness.

"I just wanted . . . to thank you," he began.

Ash looked at him for a long moment, trying to summon up some anger for what he'd almost done to her, but it wouldn't come.

"It's okay," she said.

Then she tossed the charm down.

The back of her aunt and uncle's house rose up in front of her. She was standing in the backyard. Bending down, she let the toad go. The little creature looked up at her with Nina's eyes still there in its face, for one long moment. Then it was just a toad. Ash rocked there on her heels, watching it hop off, then slowly rose to face the back of the house.

Time to go in.

Time for the new person to make a new life.

She got as far as the doorway leading into the living room and just stopped there, looking in. Her aunt and uncle were fussing over Nina. Aunt Gwen was crying and hugging Nina; Uncle John looked like he was going to cry. One of Nina's friends was there—Nina couldn't remember her name—sitting in a chair looking kind of dazed and happy, all at the same time. Cassie and Bones were there as well, as totally caught up in Nina's miraculous return as the rest of them.

Some things never changed.

Everybody was paying attention to Nina. Just like always.

Ash's hard-won resolve in the spirit-world wavered, then fled.

She wondered if they had even missed her as she turned to leave the house again.

NINA

"Ashley!" Nina cried.

Nina's whole experience in the spirit-world held a dreamlike quality for her. It was like her other dreams—she could remember it, but only at a distance. As though it had happened to someone else. The whole experience already seemed vague and lost in time.

Except for Ya-wau-tse.

And Ashley. Who'd been willing to give up everything for her.

It made Nina feel like a heel for the way she'd treated her cousin.

She saw Ashley hesitate in the doorway. Everyone else in the room moved as though in slow motion. For one long endless instant the world was just her and Ashley. The understanding that passed between them spoke volumes that could never be articulated. Then pandemonium broke loose as her mother and father rushed across the room to worry over Ashley. Her mother hugged Ashley, her father enfolded them both in his arms.

For once, Nina didn't feel an ounce of jealousy.

"Oh, you had us so scared," her mother was saying. "Don't ever do this again. Will you promise me that, Ashley? If you're not happy about something—talk to us first. Don't run away."

"I didn't run away," Ashley said. "I got taken away."

"What happened?" John asked.

As he and Gwen stepped back, Cassie moved in to give Ashley a hug.

"Lord, but you had us worried, girl," she said.

And then time was swallowed with explanations as they all told of what had happened to them that night. They were all forthcoming with each other—as though they were all friends, rather than adults and parents and children—except Ashley never spoke of how she'd saved Nina. She made it sound as though the manitou had done that. And she never spoke of the charm bracelet that hung on her left wrist. But Nina knew what it was. Her own totem still moved inside her and it let her see the world with new eyes. She could make connections between seemingly unrelated items that she'd never have thought to make before.

She knew the bracelet was magic.

Just as she knew that she and Ashley were bound together as closely as their mothers had been—for all that they were only cousins.

"Friends?" she said to her cousin when the talking was finally done.

She and Ashley were sitting on the couch with Judy between them. Nina leaned across Judy, one arm around her friend's shoulders, the other offered to Ashley.

"Friends," Ashley said, taking her hand.

"Things are going to change," Nina said.

"I hope you're going to start with your hair," Ashley said.

"What's wrong with my hair?"

"It needs a major overhaul. Really. The bangs have got to go."

"She might be right," Judy said.

"Oh, thanks a lot. Why doesn't everybody just gang up on me?"

"She's just teasing you," Judy said. "Right?"

Ashley shrugged. "Maybe . . ."

But there was a twinkle in her eyes.

"Well, what about that jacket of yours?" Nina said.

"What's wrong with my jacket?"

"What's right with it? All those headbanger patches . . ."

Nina's parents sat with Cassie and Bones on the other side

of the room, listening to the conversation. The fortune teller and her shaman friend were amused at the girls' fencing, but Gwen's brow wrinkled with worry.

"I thought they were finally going to be friends," she said. "But just listen to them."

"Maybe you should just settle on them being sisters," Cassie said.

John nodded and took his wife's hand. "I'll settle for that any day."

"Doesn't look like you have much choice," Bones said.

ASH

The next Monday afternoon after school, Ash and Nina sat together in one of the reading rooms of the G. Smithers Memorial Library at Butler University, poring over a Cornish-English English-Cornish dictionary.

"What makes you think you'll find something in that?" Nina asked.

"It's just the way she told me her name," Ash replied, running her finger down a page. "She didn't say her name *was* Lusewen; just that I could call her that. There's got to be a reason why she chose that name. Her birds both had names that meant something."

"But why're you so sure its Cornish?"

"Because that's what I am. And because the birds' names were Cornish words."

Her finger stopped in the middle of a page.

Lusewen.

It meant Ash.

"That's you," Nina said as she leaned close to reach what Ash had found.

Ash nodded.

"But what's it mean?"

Ash looked across the library, but she didn't see the long rows of bookcases, the graduate students working on their theses.

What did it mean?

It was short for Ashley.

But her extensive readings into various mystery traditions called up other meanings, meanings that were more esoteric, more . . . significant to what Lusewen represented for her.

Ash was what a fire left when it had burned right down to the heart of an object, symbolic of the transitory nature of human life. Or as the manitou might say, it reminded one of his or her life Wheel, cyclic as the seasons. A life span might seem short, but it always came around again.

Ash was also the tree in the Celtic mysteries that linked the inner and outer worlds. Yggdrasil, the World Tree from which Woden hung to gain his enlightenment. In the Ogham alphabet of the druids, Gwidion took Woden's place, and with him the mysteries lay thicker. The druids called the tree Nuin, and for them it connected the three circles of existence—which some named as the past, the present, and the future, and others as confusion, balance, and creative force.

Circles.

Wheels.

So what did that make Lusewen?

We fill the spirit-world with dreams, the manitou had told her.

Did that mean that *they* had created Lusewen as a guide for her, or was Lusewen the person that Ash could grow up to be?

I'm who you might be, Lusewen had told her the last time Ash asked her who she was.

"Ash?"

She blinked, then turned to look at her cousin.

"You looked like you were miles away," Nina said.

"I was."

She told Nina what she'd been thinking, enjoying the simple pleasure of having someone to share this kind of thing with— someone her own age, someone she could trust.

"Does that mean your totem's an ash tree?" Nina asked when she was done. "Is that kind of thing even possible?"

"I don't know."

"I wonder how can we find out for sure," Nina said.

Ash didn't reply for a long moment. She fingered the charms

on the bracelet that Lusewen had given her and then thought of the pomegranate.

She was definitely going to have to take up silverwork, she decided.

"There's only one way to find out," she said finally.

They found Bones in Fitzhenry Park, working his shtick on a tourist. They stood nearly, watching the fall of the tiny bones, the delicate way his fingers sketched their patterns in the air just above them. When he was finally done and the tourist walked away, her satisfaction expressed in the ten-dollar bill that she'd left in the wooden bowl by his knee, he turned to the girls.

"Hey, now," he said.

His clown eyes were back—mad, prancing specks dancing in their dark depths.

"Did you come by to hear the little mysteries speak through me?" he added with a grin.

Ash shook her head.

"We want you to show us how to walk the spirit-world," she said.